YES   NO

OUIJA

YES

ABCDEF

NOPQRST

12345

GOOD

JA

NO

HIJKLM
UVWXYZ
67890

BYE

For Philippa, the suffering is over.
Wait, why are your eyes all white?

Little, Brown and Company

Hachette Book Group
237 Park Avenue, New York, NY 10017
Visit us at lb-teens.com

Little, Brown and Company is a division of Hachette Book Group, Inc.
The Little, Brown name and logo are trademarks of Hachette Book Group, Inc.

The publisher is not responsible for websites (or their content)
that are not owned by the publisher.

First Edition: September 2014

Library of Congress Control Number: 2014943622

ISBN 978-0-316-29632-8

10 9 8 7 6 5 4 3 2 1

RRD-C

Printed in the United States of America

OUIJA

BY **KATHARINE TURNER**

BASED ON THE SCREENPLAY
WRITTEN BY

STILES WHITE & JULIET SNOWDEN

LITTLE, BROWN AND COMPANY
NEW YORK BOSTON

SIX YEARS BEFORE...

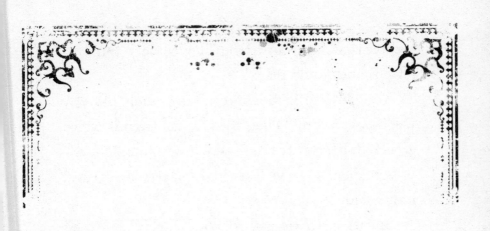

I don't know if I wanna do this."

Debbie giggled, holding her hands over the Ouija board and making spooky noises. Laine wrinkled her nose and shuffled farther away, biting the cuff of her pajamas.

"Relax, Laine," she said, smiling. "It's going to be fun. First we have to go over the rules. Never play in a graveyard. . . ."

"This is so silly." Laine sniffed, staring at the old-fashioned lettering on the board in front of her. This was not her idea of a fun sleepover, but

Debbie was her best friend; if Debbie wanted to play, Laine would play.

"You circle the board once for each player," Debbie went on. "Then we say, 'As friends we've gathered, hearts are true'—say it with me, Laine."

"As friends we've gathered, hearts are true," Laine said.

"Spirits near, we call to you." Debbie finished the rhyme with a smile.

"Spirits near, we call to you," Laine repeated dutifully.

Laine looked around at her bedroom, Debbie's sleeping bag laid out by her bed, the closet in the corner, pictures of her and Debbie at the carnival, at horseback riding camp, Debbie playing the lead in the school play. She eyed the closet again suspiciously. Had that door been open before?

"Is someone here with us?" Debbie asked.

Laine gasped as the planchette slid to YES. Debbie wiggled her eyebrows at her BFF and Laine giggled. She was being dumb. Of course it was just Debbie.

"Debbie, cut it out!" she said, giving her friend a shove. Shoving her back, Debbie picked up the heart-shaped piece of wood from the Ouija board and closed one eye, squinting at Laine through the lens in the center before she set it back on the board.

"Will Laine and I always be best friends?" she asked. "Will Laine ever get a boyfriend?"

The planchette moved over to YES once more.

"See?" Laine said. "Now I know it's fake."

"If there's a ghost in here, you can see it through the planchette," Debbie explained. "It's the eye to the other side."

She held it out to the other girl. Laine shook her head.

"I don't know," she said, feeling the weight of it in her hand.

"Relax, Laine." Debbie waggled her hands in the air. "It's just a game."

Laine raised the planchette to her blue eye and peered through the lens. She could see Debbie but the image was distorted; she looked weird and wrong.

"If someone is here with us," Debbie whispered, "make yourself known."

"Oh my gosh!" Laine screamed as the ghostly

figure of a small girl appeared in the doorway. "Debbie!"

"What are you guys doing?" the girl asked. It was Sarah, Laine's little sister.

"Get out of here, Sarah!" Laine shouted, her heart racing.

"Can I play too?" the younger girl asked, staring at the board on the floor. "What's that?"

"Go back to your room," Laine commanded, shutting the door on her sister. Sarah turned away, sulking, and marched back to her bedroom.

"Oh my God, that was freaky," Laine said, still tense, her pulse still sounding loud in her ears.

"Calm down," Debbie said, taking the planchette in her hand and tossing it up and down in the air. "It's only a game."

She brushed her long dark hair behind her ears, placing the wooden instrument back on the board....

As friends we've gathered,
Hearts are true,
Spirits near,
We call to you . . .

TWO MONTHS BEFORE...

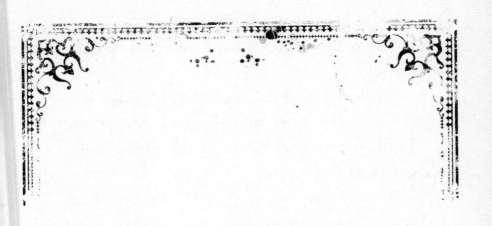

Here you are!" Laine Morris jumped out of her seat on the porch, running over to grab her best friend in a whirlwind of a hug. Her long blonde hair whipped around, catching in her eyelashes, and the other girl squealed in her ear. "You were amazing!"

"You think?" Debbie Garaldi pressed her hands against her face, realizing she had her stage makeup on, and tried wiping at a smear she'd left on Laine's shirt. "I kinda forgot my lines in the middle of my soliloquy but I covered it up okay, maybe?"

"Well, if you did, I couldn't tell," Laine said, grabbing her hand and dragging her toward Laine's front door. "Come on, superstar, everyone's waiting for you."

"Can we just wait for Pete?" Debbie asked, looking back toward the road to where a set of headlights reversed clumsily into a narrow parking spot. The excitement in Debbie's eyes softened as a tall boy in jeans and a nondescript sweater unfurled himself from the driver's side. "He's shy without me."

"He's shy with you," Laine quipped. She liked Pete—not as much as Debbie, obviously—but he was also incredibly socially awkward. "It's been, like, six months, Debs, and he still can't look at me and talk to me at the same time."

"Please, it's been seventeen years and I can hardly stand to look at you and talk to you at the same time." Debbie punched her friend in the arm gently. "I know he's not exactly the life of the party but he's just so . . ."

"Cute?" Laine finished for her friend. "And rich? And cute?"

"Well, yeah." Debbie laughed. "But I was going to say interesting."

"Okay," Laine replied as Pete loped up the street, raising a hand in a too-far-to-talk greeting. "That's what I like about Trevor too. He's *interesting*."

Debbie grinned. "You like everything about Trevor," she said in a singsong voice. "You love him, you want to marry him."

"Shut up!" Laine hissed. She flushed from head to toe, remembering she had spent all afternoon the day before watching a wedding reality show. "Get your ass inside before I cancel your party. Hey, Pete."

"S'up, Laine." Pete nodded at his girlfriend's BFF before clutching instinctively at Debbie's hand, weaving his fingers through hers. Laine turned to hide a satisfied smile as Debbie beamed up at her boyfriend. Tonight was going to be perfect.

Everyone!" Laine threw open her front door, revealing a room full of happy-looking high schoolers, dancing and talking under dim lights. "She's here!"

The room cheered, people Debbie and Laine had known all their lives rushing around to congratulate her on the play. Not that this was a rare occurrence—Debbie had been in almost every school production since kindergarten—but Laine still liked to fill the house with friendly faces when her dad was out of town for work, which was pretty much all the time since her mom had left a couple of years back. The only person who didn't look psyched to be partying sans chaperone was Laine's little sister, Sarah.

"Yo, worm," Laine called over. "What's up?"

"Nothing?" She jumped up, defensive. Sarah's black nail polish was chipped and her heavy red lipstick had a definite wannabe-rocker edge to it. It was her best attempt at rebellion while she was stuck under house arrest. "I can't even sit down without you being on my ass?"

"I'm only asking if you're okay," Laine said,

trying not to sigh. She didn't want to be a nag but her sister needed watching, constantly. It wasn't that she went looking for trouble; it was more like she'd actually invented the very concept. "You want a soda or something?"

Sarah raised an eyebrow at the punch bowl on the table. "No, Laine," she said slowly. "I don't want a *soda*. Why don't you go play with your friends and leave me alone?" Pushing through the crowd surrounding Debbie, she stomped upstairs. Because she needed to wear biker boots in the house, right?

Even though Sarah was two years younger than her sister, Laine knew she liked to think she was all grown up. Older boyfriends, cutting class, that makeup...and Laine had smelled tobacco—and worse—on her more than once. She knew it wasn't her dad's fault that he was away a lot—he needed his job to keep the family fed and times were hard out there—but she would love to stop feeling as though she had to play the stand-in mom, just for one evening.

"Let her go," a voice whispered in her ear as a

pair of strong arms wrapped around her waist. "She can't get into trouble when the house is full of people."

"You'd be amazed," Laine said, spinning around to face her boyfriend, Trevor. As soon as her eyes met his, she began to melt. "You okay?"

"I'm always okay," he said, brushing her hair out of her eyes and placing a kiss on the tip of her nose. "You don't need to worry about me. You're supposed to let me worry about you."

Laine glowed. She had to admit, that wasn't something she was used to doing. Pressing her head against Trevor's chest, she turned back to look at the party. Debbie was three people deep in hugs, her arms currently squeezing the life out of their friend Isabelle.

"Who's the guy with Iz?" Trevor asked, absently stroking Laine's hair.

Practically purring like a kitten, Laine squinted at the broad, blond-haired boy who stood awkwardly beside her friend. "No idea," she replied. "She'll have ditched him by this time next week, though, so no point trying to learn his name."

Trevor grinned. "She's an ice queen," he agreed. "Good thing she's hot."

"You think Iz is hot?" she asked, totally aware of how dumb she sounded as soon as the words came out of her mouth.

"Hell yeah," Trevor said, leaning down to rest his forehead against hers. "But not as hot as you. Or as smart. Or sweet. Or funny."

Laine pressed her lips together to stop from smiling so wide that her head fell off.

"Great ass, though," Trevor added, flinching from Laine's automatic swipe and laughing out loud. "I kid, I kid."

"She does have a great ass," Laine relented. "Thank God she's my friend or I could really hate that girl."

"Women," Trevor said, slapping Laine's own butt before heading off into the kitchen. "I will never understand you all."

"Don't pretend you're not jealous of Pete's butt," she called after him. "I've seen you looking."

Trevor lovingly flipped her off and Laine hugged herself, laughing inside. Flipping off aside, how had she gotten so lucky? Leaning against the back of the sofa, looking out at her friends, she let herself feel happy. So her mom wasn't around anymore, her dad worked long hours, and her little sister was a brat, but there, in the living room, listening to music and watching all her friends laugh and dance and smile, Laine took a mental picture and then closed her eyes so she could remember it forever. This wasn't something that could be captured on her cell phone; this was a feeling, and she hoped the feeling would last forever.

CHAPTER 1

Laine stood in front of the house, shivering in the cool evening as her cell phone burned up against her ear.

"Answer already," she muttered against the ringing, one hand on the front gate, peering into dimly lit windows. "Come on, Debbie."

As she hung up and dialed again, one of the upstairs curtains twitched and the light behind it went out. Laine took a step back and squinted into the darkness, her phone still trying to connect.

"Hey."

"Where are you?" Laine wrapped an arm around herself as her best friend's voice echoed down the line.

"I'm here," Debbie said, her voice tired and wan. "I've been here. Just been rough, you know. This week's been rough."

"You've got to tell me what's been going on." Laine tried not to sound impatient. Only she was. "And don't think you're bailing on me *again*. We're gonna be late for the game."

"Oh yeah. You know, I don't think I'm coming," Debbie said. Even though Laine knew she was inside, only a few feet away, the connection was terrible. She could barely make out the scratchy words.

"Oh yeah?" The light in the upstairs window flickered back to life and Laine waved up at her friend's silhouette. "Well, I'm not leaving until I get to talk to you."

After one second too many, Debbie moved away from the window.

"Fine. Fine. I'll come out, just gimme a sec."

Laine flung open the gate and marched up to

the front door. Debbie had been acting weird for days and now this? She dropped her cell phone into her purse and folded her arms across herself, waiting for someone to open the door. It had been a long time since that happened. Laine and Debbie always let themselves into each other's house, but just now it didn't feel right. Eventually Debbie opened the door, closing it quickly behind herself.

"What's going on with you?" Laine asked. No reason not to get straight to the point. "I didn't see you at lunch, you weren't in chem. No one could find you after school. What's up?"

"I left early," Debbie replied, her shoulders folding inward.

"Are you sick?"

Debbie stared at the floor, gnawing on her bottom lip.

Laine held back a sigh and looked over her oldest friend. Her long hair was dull and lifeless and there wasn't a trace of makeup on her face. Even with her dark eyes trained so carefully on the floor of the porch, Laine could see that they were swollen. She'd been crying.

"You and Pete have a fight?" she asked, her voice softening.

"No, nothing like that," Debbie said, shaking her head. She unfolded herself, and Laine watched as the little white fingerprints she had left on her own arms flushed bright red. "I just don't want to go out tonight."

"Then just tell me." Laine reached out to rest a hand on her arm, but Debbie pulled away, flicking her hair over her shoulder.

"It's going to sound ridiculous," she said, a sour half-laugh following her words. "It really is. You're gonna think I'm crazy."

"Hey." Laine smiled and held out her hands. "No secrets between us, remember?"

They had been best friends since before they could talk. They were closer than sisters, and there was nothing they didn't know about each other, nothing they couldn't talk about. And when you'd been best friends with someone since you were preverbal, it was easy to tell when something was seriously wrong.

Debbie took a deep breath in and let it out, slowly. "Do you remember that game we used to play when we were kids?" She scratched absently at a red mark on her neck. "Where you ask questions about the future, try to talk to . . . you know."

Laine nodded. "With the Ouija board?"

"Right?" Debbie closed her eyes, still rubbing away at the sore spot on her neck. "Couple of weeks ago, I played the Ouija. I was just messing around but . . . I don't know."

She opened her eyes, stared at Laine, desperate for an answer. "It's just a game, right?"

Laine considered her friend's confession for a moment. That was what this was about? Debbie had been messing around with some Ouija board?

"You know you've always been like this," Laine said, nodding gravely.

"Like what?" Debbie clutched at her own shirt. "Like what, Laine?"

"A total and complete dork." Laine punched her lightly on the arm. "Seriously, dude. You're freaking over a Ouija board?"

Debbie pressed her hands against her face and let out a loud, clear laugh. It rang through the air, chasing away the creepy tension that had wound itself into Laine's shoulders and setting everything straight again.

"I know, I know," Debbie said, breathing out and shaking herself down like a wet dog. "I'm just tired."

"So, I'm just gonna come in with you." Laine pulled her bag strap over her head and moved toward the front door. "I don't need to go to the game. We always lose anyway. I'll come in and we'll order pizza and—"

"No!" Debbie looked startled and threw herself into Laine's path. Laine looked at her with wide eyes as Debbie coughed, pretending to clear her throat. "I mean, my folks will be home any minute, big family-dinner plans. Wouldn't you rather hang out with Trevor than eat dinner with my parents?"

Laine gripped the strap of her bag tightly. "Now you're being weird," she said.

"I'm always being weird," Debbie reassured her, pressing her hands against Laine's shoulders, pushing her away from the door. "Go have fun. You're totally right, I'm being a dork."

Before she could argue, Laine's cell rang in the

bottom of her bag. With her eyes still locked on her twitchy best friend, she answered it.

"Hey," she said in a low voice. "I'm at Debbie's."

Debbie looked around, staring at the trees and the stars and anything other than the girl standing in front of her.

"I know," Laine said into the phone. "I'm coming. Okay, bye."

She hung up, trying not to smile.

"Trevor?" Debbie asked.

"You sure you don't want to come?" Laine asked with a slight nod. She was trying so hard not to make a big deal out of her still-new boyfriend but Debbie knew better. Debbie knew everything. "Maybe you'd feel better at the game, you know, out of the house."

"I'm good." Debbie waved away her friend's concerns but Laine knew she wasn't totally okay. "We're having leftovers for dinner and everything, it's gonna be rocking. But I'll see you in the morning, that's for sure."

"Okay, say hi to your folks for me." Laine threw her bag over her head in resignation. She really wanted to see Trevor and for whatever reason, she really wanted to get away from Debbie's house. "I'll see you at the diner?"

"If you get there first, order for me." Debbie nodded, throwing herself into a huge hug.

"Pancakes with the works," Laine said. The usual. "Got it."

Debbie smiled, her face lighting up even if her eyes didn't, and made a peace sign. Laine did the same and touched her fingers to her best friend's, the same farewell gesture they made every single day. Sometimes Trevor tried to copy it but he met empty air—even he didn't get BFF privileges. It was *their* thing. Reluctantly Laine headed down the steps to her car, looking back as Debbie hung around in the doorway.

"Love you," she called.

"Love you," Debbie repeated, blowing Laine a kiss. Laine caught it and grinned. With a tight smile, Debbie gave Laine one last wave before she closed the door.

The light in the upstairs window went out.

CHAPTER 2

Back inside the house, Debbie leaned against the kitchen counter, picking at a plate of cold chicken and staring at a hastily scribbled note from her mom. Her parents were out for the night. She pushed it to the side, wondering why she had lied to Laine. She never lied to Laine about anything.

From nowhere she heard a loud thunking sound, but she didn't jump. Weird sounds in the darkness were getting less and less weird.

Looking up, Debbie saw that the back door had blown itself open. Padding through the kitchen, she told herself that it was just the wind. Or maybe her parents had come home early? But no. The driveway was empty, her folks were still out at dinner. It was just Debbie all alone with a high night wind. Or maybe not. As she locked the door, a hissing sound breathed out behind her. She spun around to see one of the stove burners glowing blue.

"I didn't turn that on," Debbie said out loud, the sound of her voice meant to be reassuring. Instead her words rang hollow through the empty house. With shaky hands she reached to turn off the burner. It flickered out without complaint, the air around her hand still warm from the blue flame. Taking one last look around the room, she flipped off the lights and bolted out of the kitchen.

"I'm just gonna go upstairs and study," she told herself, walking quickly through the house to the stairs. "Learn my lines."

With one deep breath in, Debbie ran up the

staircase and charged into her room, closing the door behind her and switching on her lamp.

There it was.

The Ouija board sat in the middle of the room, as though it had always been there, as though she hadn't thrown it into the furnace and watched it burn. With her hand pressed against her throat, she took a step back. Every part of her was shaking and her breath was short and ragged when it came at all.

"No..." she whispered, barely able to recognize her own voice.

Why hadn't she left with Laine? Why had she stayed? Debbie took a step backward, stumbling on something underfoot. Trembling, she reached down to pick it up.

It was the planchette.

Slowly, her arm moving almost as though someone else were pushing it upward, Debbie raised the planchette to stare through the oculus in the center of the wooden heart. The thick glass distorted her empty bedroom, the wooden floor warping up toward her. And then she saw them. A pair of small filthy feet directly in front of her. Debbie screamed as they began to rush toward her, cutting off her screaming and knocking her backward. Whatever she had seen through the glass had vanished but somehow it was still there. Debbie choked, clawing at her throat, her feet scuffing against the floor and her eyes wild. Her lips began to fuse together against her silent screams and her brown eyes paled, rolling back in her head until there was nothing but white.

And then she was still.

Slowly and without a sound, Debbie yanked the Christmas lights down from her wall and calmly walked out of her room, the string of lights dragging along the floor behind her. Moonlight shone in through the kitchen windows, the note from her parents resting against her unfinished plate of leftovers. The entire house was still and quiet until a rattling noise sounded at the top of the stairs, followed by a quiet shuffling.

Without warning, Debbie dropped over the banister, one end of the Christmas lights wrapped around her throat, the other tied to a spindle on the landing. They stretched out short and tight and in a heartbeat, her neck broke with a sickening crack. Debbie swung slowly in midair, the wooden spindle creaking in mourning in the silent house.

CHAPTER 3

The next morning Laine sat in the diner, staring out the window and waiting for Debbie's Prius to pull into the parking lot. It was a regular Saturday. The basketball team sat over in the far corner, trying to work out why they had lost again last night. The drama geeks were on the other side of the room, debating whether their next show should be a musical. Laine was tucked into their usual booth, right by the counter, waiting for pancakes, coffee, Trevor, and Debbie. Same old same old.

"Hey." Trevor arrived first, sailing through the door and giving her a warm, sleepy grin before he slid into the booth beside her and kissed her cheek. "Sorry I'm late. I have a surprise for you."

"Ooh, you have a map." Laine returned his smile, switching her attention from the busy parking lot to the map he had laid out on the table. "This is very intriguing. I am officially intrigued."

"This is the place," he said, combing his shaggy dark blond hair away from his face. "Up the coast, away from everyone. We make camp right about here, hike down to the beach anytime we want."

Laine's ears pricked up. "This is the first time I'm hearing a 'we' in your big plan."

Trevor folded up the map and shrugged, a pair of adorable dimples betraying his casual attitude. "I want you to come with me."

"But this was your big camping trip with the guys," Laine said, trying not to look too excited. They'd been dating for only a few months and he'd been planning this trip forever. Ditching his buddies for his girlfriend was a bold move. They were definitely going to give him a lot of grief for it, and she couldn't have been happier about it.

"I know." He wrapped his arm around her shoulders. "But I started thinking about it and I realized I'd miss you too much."

Laine sighed happily. She had been nursing a crush on Trevor since he'd transferred two years ago. It wasn't like she was unpopular, she and Debbie were pretty tight with most of the different groups without really committing to any one in particular, but Trevor was something else. He was tall enough to play ball, smart enough to make the honor roll, and cute enough to start an all-out war in the girls' locker room after one super-fraught game of dodgeball. He was the hot, sexy surfer type, all brooding and mysterious, and Laine hadn't thought she stood a chance. Then, one morning a few months ago, she'd literally run into him while he was walking his dog in the woods near her house. After the world's most awkward and sweaty conversation, they started running into each other almost every day: in the woods, at school, at the diner. And before she knew it, they were inseparable.

"So you're surfing all day." Laine leaned into her boyfriend and felt his warmth spread all the way through her body. "And what do I do?"

"I'm gonna teach you," he said, tucking the folded map into the back pocket of his jeans. "By the end of the week, you'll be one with the waves. It'll be awesome, right? Forget about the world for a while, your dad, your sister. Leave it all behind, just me and you."

"Sounds nice," Laine replied, her mind spinning out over all the things they could do when it was just the two of them, alone. "I can't wait to see you run this past my dad."

Trevor winked. "Got that figured out. I'll tell him it's the senior trip. Fully chaperoned."

"Good luck with that." Laine laughed.

"I can be persuasive," he said, his lips close to her ear.

"Really?"

"Yeah," he whispered. "I've been told."

"By who exactly?" she asked, before Trevor cut her off with a soft, warm kiss.

If there was one thing on earth that could distract Trevor from kissing Laine, it was the smell of bacon. Three plates of food were expertly tossed across the table, each one full of warm, fluffy pancakes and crunchy, crackling strips of pig.

"Hey, you two." Isabelle, waitress extraordinaire and one of Laine's best friends, cleared her throat to interrupt the make-out session. "Break it up."

Laine smiled, clutching Trevor's hand underneath the table.

"Yo, Iz." Trevor pushed his coffee cup across the table to the tired-looking Isabelle. "Little more bean juice?"

Isabelle refilled all four cups on the table, and then slid into the booth opposite Laine, grabbing a strip of bacon from Debbie's plate.

"Where's Debbie?" Iz asked, brandishing her stainless steel coffee jug. Laine looked out at the parking lot one more time, but there was still no sign of Debbie's car. "I got her food already."

"She's just running late," Laine said, ignoring Iz's typical short tone and hoping she was right. She hadn't felt right leaving Debbie alone last night, and at last count she'd sent six texts that had gone unanswered. Not that it was strange for

Debbie to lose her phone, but still, something felt off.

"So, what time are we hitting that party tonight?" she asked, tightening her long dark brown ponytail. "I can't wait to get home and shower this place off me."

"Mmm." Laine rested her head on Trevor's shoulder, ignoring Isabelle's rolling eyes. "I think we're passing."

"Yeah," he agreed, sipping his coffee. "Might watch a movie or something."

"No! You guys can't ditch the party!" Isabelle slapped the table with both hands and gave her friends her most resolute expression. "I gotta go out. Laine, he's making you bail on me. Think of the sisterhood."

"You're a big girl, Iz." Trevor laughed, slapping her hand away from a second strip of bacon. "Nothing wrong with flying solo."

Isabelle shook her head. "Showing up alone is not a good look for me," she said, waving wildly at the two of them. "Not everyone has this, you know."

"Wait." Laine copied Iz's hand gesture with a grin. "What is 'this,' anyhow?"

"Your perfect-couple situation," she replied with a sigh. "I hate you guys."

"Look at her," Laine said, theatrically ignoring her friend. "Acting like she's not the one who breaks up with every guy she goes out with."

"Can't help it." Iz smirked behind her coffee cup. "I'm a picky bitch."

No one was rushing to argue when Laine's cell phone buzzed into life in the middle of the table.

"What's up?" Trevor rubbed his hand down her back as Laine scrunched up her face at the text.

"From my dad," she said, scooting along the booth and jumping to her feet. "I gotta go."

"Let me guess, your sister?"

"No doubt," Laine replied, giving him a quick kiss on the cheek and throwing Isabelle a wave. "Causing chaos wherever she goes. Family drama strikes again. Tell Debbie to text me when she shows?"

Heading out to her car, Laine cursed her sister for costing her some quality Trevor time, not to mention a plateful of pancakes and bacon. What was it going to take for her to grow up?

As predicted, Laine found her sister on the sofa, hands pressed against her knees, feet pressed together, and more makeup on her face than you would find at the average drugstore.

"All right, worm." Laine tossed her bag on the armchair, sticking her hands on her hips. "What'd you do this time?"

Sarah looked up at her sister, her heavily lined eyes full of tears. "It's not me," she whispered, her voice cracking as she spoke.

"Dad?" Laine looked up to see her dad standing in the kitchen. Sarah wasn't the only one who had been crying. "What's wrong?"

"Elaine, you should sit down," he said, starting toward his oldest daughter, phone in hand and arms outstretched.

"I don't want to sit down," she said, her voice getting louder as she backed away. In the kitchen she could see Nona, her and Sarah's former nanny, wiping her eyes at the table. This all felt far too familiar. A rerun of when her mom left them. "What happened? Nona, what are you doing here?"

"*Nieta.*" Nona stood up, wringing her hands in lieu of an answer. "I'm so sorry."

It was too much. "Sorry for what? What's going on?" Laine shouted.

"Nona wanted to be here for you," her dad explained, inching forward. "It's Debbie."

Her dad was still talking but Laine didn't need to hear anything else; she already knew what had happened. She could feel it. She couldn't think. She couldn't breathe. Sarah, Nona, everything began to swim in front of her eyes. Debbie. There had been an accident. Debbie had been in an accident...sort of. The last thing she saw was her dad rushing across the room to catch her as she collapsed onto the living room floor.

CHAPTER 4

Standing on the steps outside Debbie's house, Laine paused for a moment and felt her black skirt whip around her legs. It was the right kind of day for a funeral, if there was such a thing. The sky was gray and miserable and even though the wind made a few attempts to kick up a fuss, it never quite managed to make itself known.

"I don't think I can do this," Laine whispered, holding on to the porch. This was the last place she had spoken to Debbie, the last place Debbie had spoken to anyone. "It doesn't feel real. She should still be here."

A warm, weathered hand found its way into hers and squeezed softly. "The day I started working for your family," Nona said, weaving an arm around Laine's waist and pulling her gently toward the door, "you introduced me to Debbie and said you only had one rule, that she was always welcome." The older woman met Laine's eyes with a smile she couldn't return. "When you have loved someone with all your heart, then a part of them is always there when you need them to guide you. I believe these are the real angels, hold on to this, *Nieta*."

Laine looked away, tears scratching at the corners of her eyes. She hadn't stopped crying since she'd heard the news; it was a miracle that she had any tears left. Nona pressed her other hand against Laine's heart and gave her a decisive nod.

"She's right here."

Laine blew out a heavy breath and mirrored Nona's nod, allowing herself to be drawn into the house. Everyone said she would feel better after the funeral, everyone said it would help her move on, only she didn't *want* to move on. She wanted to go back to Friday night, tell Trevor she wasn't coming to the game, and stop Debbie from doing what she did.

Everyone else was already inside, Laine noted as she walked through the house like a zombie, wiping away tears as Nona guided her through to the living room. Isabelle and Trevor huddled around the fireplace, smiling weakly, neither one of them knowing what to say. Instead of speaking, Trevor wrapped Laine in a big hug, kissing the top of her head. Sarah followed her sister into the house and hugged Isabelle, weeping silently.

"I just don't understand," Laine said, her voice muffled against Trevor's chest.

"None of us do," Trevor replied. "No one does."

"She told me," Laine said, pulling away and looking into his eyes for answers that she knew he didn't have. "She told me she'd see us the next morning. Why would she say that if she was going to . . ."

Her voice trailed off into nothing, unable to say the words.

"We're never going to know," Sarah told her sister, still holding on to Isabelle. "She's gone. That's what happens."

"I wish she would have talked to us," Iz mumbled, her heart breaking in her voice. "About whatever it was."

Laine shook her head, looking around at the familiar room that looked so strange. "I know what the police said but I can't believe she'd ever..."

Over on the sofa, Debbie's mom and dad clutched at each other, their smart black outfits crumpled by grief. Laine stared. She had no idea what to say to them. Why hadn't they been home when it happened? Why hadn't they been there to save her?

Don't get angry, she reminded herself silently. *It's not their fault that Debbie is...*

Rather than finish the thought in her own mind, she wandered closer to Debbie's mom and dad, tuning in to the conversations all around her.

"...and that Carol had to find her like that." A tall blonde woman stood by the fireplace, glass in one hand, crushed-up tissue in the other.

Laine stared at her blankly. "They're packed and coming to stay with me," she continued. "Carol can't possibly be in this house another night."

Laine hovered, eyes narrowing at this woman. How dare she talk about Debbie? And who was she anyway? How could someone Laine didn't even recognize think she could swoop in and take care of everything? Shaking her head, she moved away, over to a quiet spot by the window. She couldn't keep getting angry like this; it wasn't anyone's fault. Not any more than it was hers, at least.

Just as she was about to make her excuses and leave, Laine caught sight of a lanky guy standing in the doorway. He stood tall in his suit, the crisp lines and expensive material contradicting his messy haircut, and he was holding a sad-looking bouquet of flowers that had not enjoyed their journey over.

"Pete," Laine said, holding up a hand by way of a hello.

"Laine." Debbie's boyfriend lifted his eyes to meet hers, but his expression didn't change. He must have been in this house a hundred times, but he looked like he had never set foot through the door before. "Hey."

"I'm so sorry," Laine said, just for something to say. It seemed to be what everyone else was going with.

Pete nodded, looking down at the bouquet in his hand. "I brought flowers. Debbie liked this kind."

"Yeah," Laine agreed, touching one of the petals lightly. "They're really pretty. I can put them in some water if you want?"

"No." Pete sniffed back an errant tear. "I'll go find her mom. I should give them to her."

Laine nodded, wondering whether she should go with him. She hadn't spoken to Mrs. Garaldi since it had happened. It would make the whole thing way too real. She watched Pete approach the couch and saw him swallowed up in a sea of mourners, a fresh wave of sobbing overwhelming all six feet of him. Turning her back on the wake, Laine disappeared up the staircase, away from all of it.

Debbie's room looked exactly as it always had. There was no black sheet pulled over the window, no police tape at the door. Shouldn't something change when someone died? Her online profile had already been turned into a memorial, her locker was covered in photos and flowers and notes—who had done those things? Shouldn't they do the same to her room? But no, it looked just the same as ever, like Debbie was about to run in, late getting home from date night with Pete, ready to video-chat all the juicy details with Laine before bed.

Laine stood right in the middle of the room and stared out the window. The only thing missing was the string of Christmas lights that usually lit up the mural of a tree Debbie had painted on her wall. Laine fought back a wave of nausea when she remembered why the lights were missing. She pressed her hand over her mouth and choked on a sob. Debbie wasn't the kind of person who would do that.

But now Debbie wasn't anything. And without Debbie, Laine had no idea who she was. The bedroom walls were covered in photographs of camping trips and birthdays, varsity pins and corsages from prom dresses, playbills, posters, and every last damn movie ticket from the last seventeen years. *Debbie kept everything*, Laine thought, almost smiling. She had been such a hoarder. Almost every single photo was of the two of them, except a couple of more recent shots of Debbie and Pete.

Something inside the closet behind her clattered to the floor, making Laine jump and knocking the door open.

"You were everything to her."

A voice in the doorway made Laine spin around on her heel. It was Debbie's mom, a tight smile plastered across her face.

"Mrs. G," Laine said, her heart in her throat. She'd been dreading this. "I'm sorry. I just...I just wanted to be in her room."

All day she'd managed to keep it together. Silent tears, zombielike wandering, handshakes, awkward hugs...but it was all too much. Here in Debbie's room, face-to-face with her mother, Laine felt her control slipping away. The tears started quietly but before she knew it, every part of her was shaking with uncontrollable, heaving sobs. Debbie's mom rushed across the room, wrapping her in a hug that she'd known her whole life. Finally Laine's tears slowed and softened and she relaxed into Mrs. G's arms.

"The hours you two spent in here," she said, breaking away and holding Laine at arm's length. "When you girls were little, sometimes I'd stand outside the door and listen to you talk. Couldn't help myself, you know? I loved hearing your conversations. All the plans you made for the future. You already had your college picked out in fifth grade."

"Debbie even drew pictures of what our dorm room would look like." Laine nodded. "Only everything was purple."

"I remember that." Mrs. Garaldi laughed. A fluttering, unreliable sound. "God, do I remember her purple phase."

They smiled at each other, sharing the moment in silence. Laine could have sworn she actually felt her heart break in two.

"And then you both got in. Just like you planned."

Suddenly Mrs. Garaldi jerked her hands away and slammed them down by her sides. It was too much. With a loud sniff she looked up at the smoke alarm on the ceiling, then picked up a purple fabric-covered box and started grabbing random items from around the room. Laine watched, speechless, as she added one thing after another to the strange collection—a bracelet, Debbie's key ring, an old mini video camera, photos pulled right from the wall.

"Mrs. G..." Laine started, with no idea of what to say next.

"She'd want you to have these," Debbie's mom replied, handing her the box and ushering her out of the room and closing the door. "Always remember her, Laine, always remember her."

CHAPTER 5

Oh, that's the one," Debbie said. "Very hot, lemme see that booty shake!"

"Yeah?" Laine replied, dropping her hips in her best pop-star impression. "You like this?"

"Ladies, I need you to keep it down in there," the disembodied voice of the salesperson called outside the changing room. "We do have other customers."

Both girls cracked up and the tiny screen on the video camera in Laine's hand cut to a new scene. Tucked up in her bed, she wiped away tears, holding Debbie's mini video camera steady under the covers as their recent shopping trip turned into a view of their high school. Debbie's smiling face was front and center, Pete's confused expression hovering in the corner of the screen.

"Little kiss for the camera," Pete said, trying to press his lips to Debbie's cheek while still holding the camera. Clearly Debbie had not schooled him in the ways of the selfie.

"Pete, stop." She laughed before the screen switched to Laine and Debbie standing in the Garaldis' foyer, posing in their formal dresses. Before Laine could react, the scene changed one last time. Debbie held the camera out as far as she could, throwing her other arm around Laine's neck and pulling her into the shot. That night had been the best. It had been before Debbie was dating Pete, before Laine had even made eye contact with Trevor. Before Sarah had started to get into trouble, before her mom had left town. And Laine would have traded every second of it just to say hi to Debbie one more time. She wondered if Debbie had been working on a greatest hits video for them—she did stuff like that all the time.

She closed the camera, placing it carefully back in her box of memories. Her laptop glowed beside her in the darkness, showing Debbie's page. It refreshed every couple of minutes, someone else posting a photo, leaving a message of condolence. Laine combed carefully through the box, sliding Debbie's bracelet onto her wrist, dangling a tiny penguin keychain from her finger. She swung it back and forth, tipping her head to one side to consider his little sunglasses, when she realized the car engine she could hear outside wasn't moving. Placing all Debbie's things back inside the box, she looked out the window to see an old beater turning out its headlights a few houses up the street. It wasn't the first time she'd seen that car.

With a frustrated sigh, Laine clambered off her bed as her sister's door quietly clicked open.

"Really, Sarah?" She looked her little sister up and down. "After everything that's happened today? You're doing this?"

Sarah stuck out her chin and crossed her arms across her low-cut shirt. "Doing what?"

"Sneaking out?" Laine hissed. Their dad had passed out on the couch hours ago. Working all the overtime he could get was hard enough; the last thing he needed was to deal with another of Sarah's mini rebellions. "Making things so hard all the time?"

"I need to get outta here," Sarah replied, her black eyeliner already smudging underneath her eyes. "Try to forget this crappy day ..."

Who'd had the bad day here?

"Sorry, but you're not going anywhere." Laine blocked her sister's path. "Not tonight."

"Um, Mom's not around?" Sarah waved her arms around the hallway, as though Laine might not have noticed their mother's absence. "Hasn't been for a long time. You're not her, it's not your job to hover all over me."

"I wish I didn't have to," Laine whisper-yelled.

"Then just don't care so much," Sarah said, bumping past her sister on her way down the stairs. "It's way easier. I can't wait until you're gone next year."

"Sarah, get back in your room." Their dad hadn't been as fast asleep as either of them thought. Sarah let out an angry little yelp and hurled herself back down the hall.

"Nice, Laine," she grunted. "Look what you did. I would have been gone by now."

"I heard the car coming," Mr. Morris yelled up the stairs. "I know that's the guy you've been skipping school with. What the hell is going on with you, Sarah?"

"Why is everyone always up in my business?" she shouted, slamming her bedroom door shut behind her.

"Because I'm getting calls at work," Mr. Morris replied, running up the stairs and shouting through the black bedroom door. "The principal says one more no-show and you're getting expelled. Do you even understand what that means?"

Feeling her face crumpling in on itself, Laine slid back into her room and closed the door on the raised voices, listening to them through the wall. It wasn't the first time she'd heard her dad and sister have this argument—it likely wouldn't be the last. When her mom went away to a conference in Vermont and never came home, it was

Debbie who had slept in Laine's bed every night until she could go more than three hours without waking up in fits of tears. It was Debbie who had helped out around the house, making casseroles, and she and Mrs. Garaldi who had driven Sarah to and from her swim meets, before she quit of course. Laine's dad always told her she was the glue that held the family together, but she wasn't really. It was Debbie who had kept her going, and now she didn't know what to do without her.

CHAPTER

6

Dad!" Laine ran out to the street just in time to catch the taxi before it pulled away. "You forgot your flight confirmation."

"Ah, thanks, honey," he said, sticking his head out the car window and smiling. "Once the permits get approved, we'll do something fun, all three of us. It's going to be a few days, though."

Laine nodded, a tight smile stretched across her face. She didn't want her dad to leave but she couldn't tell him why. It had been such a strange day. She had walked around in a daze, sitting in class with Isabelle, neither of them speaking more than two words to the other all day long, and when she saw Sarah in the hall, her sister's eyes had been red and raw. She'd passed Pete at lunch but been unable to muster more than a wave, and the one time she ran into Trevor, he had ignored her completely.

"Nona knows I'm gone." Mr. Morris folded up the piece of paper she had handed him and slid it into his jacket pocket. "Call her if you need anything at all."

"I got it covered," Laine said, her smile beginning to falter. If only he would just leave.

As the driver began to pull away, her dad fastened his seat belt and gave her a grin. "You're the one who holds us all together, you know that, right?" he called as the taxi drove away. "Love you, kiddo."

"Love you too, Dad," Laine said, hugging herself and watching the car disappear around the corner.

The Garaldis' front gate always needed oiling but Mr. Garaldi was always too busy to take care of it. Laine rested her hand on the wood, swinging it back and forth very slightly.

"I know Mrs. G asked for help while they're gone," Trevor said, covering her hand with his. "But we can find someone else."

Laine shook her head, pushing the gate open. "If that pool cover goes into the drain and burns up the filter motor, it could really—"

"It doesn't *have* to be you," Trevor interrupted her. "That's all I'm saying. And it really shouldn't be you alone. I wish you'd told me you were doing this sooner."

"I want to, Trevor," she said with a half-smile. She wouldn't have made it through the last few days if it hadn't been for him. "Every time I walk in there, I think I'm going to see her. I guess I have to start realizing that I'm not."

Trevor tilted his head to one side, his mouth sliding into a sympathetic frown. "Maybe just focus on remembering the good stuff," he suggested.

"I tried," Laine replied, pushing the gate open and pulling the spare key from her jeans pocket.

"I watched videos of her. She just seemed so alive, so happy."

They reached the front door and Laine stopped. "What could change all of that? And why wouldn't she tell me?"

Trevor shook his head. There weren't any answers he could give her, no matter how much he would like there to be.

"You want to take the pool?" she asked, one hand on the front door. "I'm on mail duty."

Trevor gave her a quick salute, kissed her on the top of her head, and jogged around to the back of the house. Laine touched her hair where he had kissed her and smiled sadly. Every time he did that she felt her heart knit itself back together a fraction, and then in the next second she remembered what had happened to Debbie and it was torn apart all over again.

She let herself into the house, pushing a pile of mail against the wall. Most of it looked like sympathy cards, a couple of newspapers, an electric bill. Stacking it all on a side table, Laine walked through the living room to the dining room. No one had really cleaned up after the wake. Coffee cups sat around staining themselves and there was an open tin of cookies on the kitchen counter. Mrs. G would never have left cookies out on the counter; she lived in mortal fear of mice. They must have really wanted to get out of town.

Filling up a pitcher of water, Laine moved wearily around the downstairs, watering every plant she came across. She was always tired these days, but at night she couldn't sleep. She paused by the kitchen window, watching as Trevor got down on his belly by the pool, reaching for the windblown cover. She held her breath until she saw him grab it, fasten it, and stand, unharmed.

"Hurry up, Trevor," she said out loud, resting the empty pitcher back in the sink. "I'm ready to go."

Laine was at the bottom of the stairs, checking her back pocket for the key, when she heard it. A slow, heavy dragging sound came from upstairs, followed by three distinct bumps. She stepped back, staring up into the darkness, but there was nothing there. *What the hell was that?*

"Somebody there?" she called out. "Hello?"

Laine climbed the stairs and saw the light in Debbie's room was on. *Weird*, she thought; she could have sworn it hadn't been lit when she came in. It flickered on and off for a moment, until Laine pushed open the door into a darkened, empty room.

The lamp beside Debbie's bed suddenly came to life, flickering on and off as though the bulb were loose. Laine reached inside the shade and tightened it, then turned the switch to make sure it was off. The bulb was cold even though it had just been lit up. Turning to leave, she noticed the closet door was slightly ajar. There was a small wooden heart on the floor. She reached down and picked it up, studying the glass lens in its center.

"Where did you come from?" she whispered, reaching up into the closet and feeling around among the sweaters until she found something long and flat and smooth. Curious, she pulled whatever it was out of the closet and held it up to the dim afternoon light coming in through the window.

It was an old Ouija board.

"Hey." Trevor appeared in the doorway.

"Oh my God." Laine gripped the board tightly. "You almost gave me a heart attack."

"Just me." He grinned. "You ready to go?"

Laine nodded, holding the board in her hands. "Yeah. I didn't even hear you come inside. The sound in this house always carries."

"What's that?" Trevor asked, eyeing Laine's bounty.

"Something Debbie and I used to do," she replied. "Ages ago."

"Oh, man." Trevor tilted his head and smiled in recognition. "So hokey."

"I know," Laine said, pushing her hair over one shoulder and wiping the board with the sleeve of her sweater. "But we pretended it was real, you know?"

She went over to the bed and placed the Ouija board down beside her, resting her fingertips on the planchette, and gestured for Trevor to come over.

"You ask questions and the board answers," she explained as he sat down at her side. "Like, do I have a secret admirer or will we be friends forever."

"It's such a chick thing," he said. "It's just one of you pushing it around."

Laine looked up at Trevor and lightly pushed the planchette until it was resting on the word YES in the corner of the board.

"I didn't know she still had this one," she said. She pulled her hand away and rested it carefully on her knee, her voice barely above a whisper. "Debbie was acting so strange the night she died. I can't believe she's gone. If I had stayed...I was right here. If I hadn't left her, you know?"

"No, Laine," he said, closing his hand around hers. "It wasn't your fault, okay? You can't for a second think that. It's not fair to do that to yourself."

Laine shook her head, tightening her fingers around his. "You don't know when it's going to be the last time you talk to someone. I never even got to say good-bye."

Trevor put his arms around her for a second before pulling her to her feet. It felt so good but she couldn't relax the way she used to, the way she wanted to. "I know," he said, one eye on the Ouija board. "C'mon, we should go."

Laine nodded, breaking off the hug and picking up the board to put it down on Debbie's desk. It didn't feel right, leaving anything on her bed.

"Ready?" Trevor hung from the doorframe, itching to leave.

"Ready," Laine agreed, sliding the planchette over to the bottom of the board, resting it on the words GOOD BYE.

CHAPTER 7

Pete?"

Laine tapped the tall, messy-haired boy on the shoulder, making him jump.

"Can you talk?" she asked. Pete looked around as though he were checking with his friends, but he was completely alone. Not unusual for Pete. He had transferred in from a private school a couple of years ago and had never really adjusted. The only person he had ever been truly close to was Debbie. The rest of their class moved around them, slowly making their way into school.

"Yeah." He hitched his backpack up onto his shoulder and gave Laine his best attempt at a smile. "Sure."

"Haven't gotten a chance to really talk to you," Laine said, moving uncomfortably from foot to foot. "You doing okay?"

"I guess?" Pete replied, holding his phone. "I keep listening to her voice mails, can't bring myself to erase them. It's like she's still here, you know? Calling me, making plans . . ." His sentence drifted off into nothing.

Laine took a deep breath and steeled herself to ask her awkward questions. "Before Debbie died," she began. "Did you notice anything going on with her?"

"Like what?" he asked.

"Acting different?"

Pete hesitated for a moment before nodding slowly. "Yeah, she seemed worried about something."

"She ever say what it was?" Laine brushed her long hair behind her ears. She had really been hoping that Pete would be able to reassure her, not make her feel worse.

"It just kind of started out of nowhere, a few weeks ago maybe," he said, suddenly very interested in his own fingernails. "I'd text her and she'd blow me off. I guess maybe I thought she wanted to break up or something."

Now Laine knew something was up. Debbie had loved Pete completely; if that thought had even crossed his mind, she had definitely been hiding something.

"A few days ago I went to her house to try to talk to her?" Pete went on. "She didn't even want me to come inside."

"She did the same thing to me," Laine said. Damn it. If only she hadn't been so wrapped up in Trevor, maybe she would have noticed that something was really wrong.

Pete looked over at Laine. They were friendly but it wasn't like they were best friends. This whole dynamic felt so weird without Debbie in the middle of the two of them.

"Why are you asking me all this?" he said finally.

"I don't know." Laine shrugged. "Guess I'm not ready to let her go."

"Me neither."

The bell rang loudly and the last few straggling students began dragging themselves up the steps.

"I gotta head in," Pete said, tipping his head toward the door.

Laine nodded, meeting his eyes but not moving. School didn't seem important compared to the gnawing feeling in her stomach. Something had been really wrong with Debbie and she needed to know what it was.

It was late when Laine heard the laughter in her room. Somewhere between dreams there was a faint giggle that sounded just like Debbie's. She opened her eyes and listened hard. There it was again. Great, she wasn't dreaming, she was just going crazy. Reaching over to switch on her lamp, Laine rubbed her eyes, searching the room for the source of Debbie's laughter. Facedown in the middle of the floor was the camera with the screen open, playing by itself. It showed the two of them at the dance, right where Laine had turned it off, the two girls throwing each other around the room, doubled over laughing.

Laine curled up in bed and watched the video, the reality of it all washing over her. Debbie was gone, really gone, and Trevor was right—it had been an accident. If things had been the other way around, Laine wouldn't want Debbie hiding away in her room, walking around like a zombie and ignoring all her friends.

Without warning, the screen on the video camera switched to a different scene. This time it was just Debbie, seemingly alone in her room but talking to someone.

"Talking to herself again," Laine whispered into her pillow with a pang.

"I wish you were here so that we could talk about it," she said, straight into the camera. Laine shivered. It was as though Debbie were talking directly to her. "That game we used to play as kids."

Laine sat up, pulling her duvet around her.

"I did something I shouldn't have. I think I broke a rule. One rule at least, maybe more."

Unable to stay still, Laine pushed away her covers and clambered out of bed, over to where the box of trinkets Mrs. Garaldi had given her sat on her desk.

"I was just messing around," Debbie said, "but this time it felt different. Not like when we were kids and we'd, like, play at, like, a friend's sleepover or whatever. I don't know, this time it just felt like...I made contact with someone out there. I don't know. I need to play again to make sure I'm not losing my mind."

CHAPTER 8

I can't explain this," Laine said, resting her head in her hands, elbows slipping on the Formica table of their usual booth at the diner. Trevor and Iz kept their eyes on her as she searched for the words. "It's like she's there."

"Laine, listen," Trevor said, pushing his hair out of his face, frustrated. "Everyone's still in shock, okay? But those things you were telling me the other day, about feeling guilty? You don't have to keep doing this to yourself. None of this is your fault."

Laine sighed. She knew he was trying to help but he just wasn't listening. "You ever feel like even after someone you love has died, there's still a way to talk to them?" she asked Isabelle.

"You want to talk to Debbie?" Iz asked. Laine looked at the two of them and nodded.

"But you can't do that," Trevor said, confused. "She's gone."

"The board," Laine explained. "The one I found in Debbie's room. Isn't that what you're supposed to do with it?"

"But yesterday you said it was just a game," Trevor pointed out. "It's not real."

"So if we play the game and nothing happens, then I'll never bring it up again," Laine bargained. Isabelle looked at her, unsure and uncomfortable. "But I really want to try, so . . . will you guys just do this with me?"

Trevor looked at Iz, Iz looked at Trevor, and they both looked at Laine.

"I'm in," Isabelle said, getting up and retying

her apron. "I gotta get back to work." She reached out and rested her hand on Laine's shoulder, offering her a smile. Laine smiled back and squeezed her friend's hand before Iz vanished back through the kitchen doors.

Laine and Isabelle had not started out as the best of friends. In fact, Iz hadn't started out as anyone's friend. Bossy, bitchy, and superior, she had been thrown together with Laine as her partner on a science project, much to Laine's dismay, but there was only so long you could give the silent treatment to someone when you were cutting up fetal pigs together. One long afternoon in the lab and two cappuccinos later, Laine couldn't imagine not having Iz in her life. Sure, she could still be a little difficult and always knew best, but life as an army brat had made her tough. Why bother making friends when you never knew which school you'd be going to in September, she'd said one time. Of course, that was before her dad's accident, and now Iz had gotten her wish to settle down, just not the way she'd wanted to.

"Me too," Trevor said. "Whatever it takes to make you feel better."

Laine settled back in the booth, leaning into her boyfriend. Whatever it took, she was going to get through to Debbie on the other side and find out what had really happened.

CHAPTER

9

Laine, it's Dad, I'm working late."

Again, thought Laine as she listened to her dad's voice mail message. "You guys go ahead and eat without me. And just keep an eye on Sarah, okay? See you in the morning, love you."

Awesome. Keep an eye on Sarah. Exactly what she didn't need this evening. Laine jogged downstairs to find her little sister on the couch. Studying.

"Hey," she said, surprised. "I have to run out, so I'm dropping you off at Nona's."

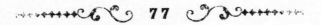

"Laine, I'm totally in the middle of this." Sarah's voice had more than a hint of a whine in it. "Dad put me on notice, so look, I'm studying. Leave me alone."

It sure looked as if she was studying. Chem books, notepads, three different colors of highlighter.

"One hour and I'll be back," Laine said, fastening her hair in a high ponytail and grabbing her keys from the table. "There's some dinner stuff in the fridge. Sarah, do you hear me?"

"One hour," she replied without even looking up from her book. "I got it. Later."

With one last look, Laine headed out the front door, nervously squeezing the plastic water bottle in her left hand. It was almost seven already; the others would be at Debbie's house by now.

"What is that noise?" she wondered, a loud, heavy thumping coming from down the street. But there was nothing mysterious about this. Three, four houses down she spotted the same beat-up black car she'd seen outside their house a dozen times.

"Hey," she shouted, jogging toward the car. "I see you!"

Pulling her arm back, she threw the water bottle as hard as she could. It landed on the hood at the exact same time the car turned its lights on, revved its engine, and peeled away up the street.

"What the hell?"

Laine turned to see her sister storming out of their house.

"For a minute there, I actually had a little faith in you," she said, furious. When would Sarah learn? What would it take?

"We hang out," Sarah shouted. "What's so wrong with that?"

"What's wrong is that you're fifteen," Laine pointed out, throwing her arms up into the air. "And that dude should know better. You know what, since you can't be left alone, you're coming with me."

Sarah crossed her arms and stamped a bare foot. "I'm not going anywhere."

Laine looked at the ground, all the fire burning out in her belly. "You know what?" she said. "I'll let Dad deal with it. I think he said if you messed up again—at all—you'd have to go to that special school. You know, the one where they send problem kids?"

Sarah's angry expression slipped to show slight concern.

"I'm sure it's nice." Laine started walking toward her car. "Oh, but remember, when you have to use pepper spray on your classmates, hold your arm away from your face. *Away.*"

Sarah pouted for a moment before turning back toward the house. "I'm getting my jacket."

"That's what I thought," Laine said. "Go get that jacket."

CHAPTER 10

Sarah and Laine pulled up outside Debbie's house ten minutes later and found Trevor and Isabelle waiting on the porch. They nodded, half-smiling at Sarah, but no one said a word until Laine had unlocked the door and stepped inside.

"I don't want to be in this house," Iz said, hugging her arms around herself. "It feels wrong."

"This is where Debbie died," Laine replied, trying to sound strong even though she felt exactly the same. "We have to play here. It's okay, we're all here together."

"Okay, so where are we doing this?" Sarah asked. Laine had given her the short version of events on the way over and she was kind of excited. She'd never played with a Ouija board before.

"Dining room," Laine said, pointing toward the big round table. It almost glowed in the moonlight. "I'm going to get the board."

Isabelle hovered in the doorway miserably as Laine vanished upstairs.

"How are you gonna talk to someone with a game?" Sarah asked Trevor, her voice just a whisper. "'Yo, Debbie, can you hear me now? Signal's bad, I'm only getting, like, one bar in here.'"

"Your sister needs to do this," Trevor replied, giving Sarah a stern look. "So just zip it up and go along."

Sarah laughed to herself, walking away into the dining room as Trevor started turning on some lights. With an air of resignation, Isabelle tiptoed into the dining room, reaching out to turn on the lamp in the corner. Without warning, a tall, shadowy figure moved out of the corner of the room.

"Jesus," she shrieked. "Pete."

Pete hit the light switch on the wall and a warm golden glow swept over the room from the lamp. Isabelle held her hand to her chest, panting, while Trevor turned to stare down the other guy, his face creased in anger.

"What the hell are you doing, man?" Trevor raised his voice, shattering the tension in the room.

"Nice to see you too, Trevor," Pete replied smoothly.

"Nicer to see you," Trevor said. "You trying to creep us out or what?"

"You knew I was coming."

"Yeah, but we all agreed to meet outside." Trevor shook his arms, as if to shake off the adrenaline running through his body.

"I have the spare key for the back door." Pete held up a small, shiny silver object. "I always let myself in."

Trevor bit back his response. He was already on edge, and this didn't need to turn into a fight. He took a deep breath and walked over to the table. The sooner this was over the better. He'd never say anything to Laine but he'd never been Pete's biggest fan. The guy was always hovering on the edges of conversations, speaking barely above a whisper in that high-class, private-school-educated voice. And there was something about his stance, like he was always ready to bolt at any second.

"Are you ready?" Laine asked, appearing at the bottom of the stairs, clutching the board to her chest. Without a word Trevor, Isabelle, Sarah, and Pete took their seats at the dining table.

Laine put the board down on the table, placed the planchette in the center, and carefully laid a black-and-white photograph of Debbie next to the board. Isabelle looked away, nervously braiding and unbraiding her hair.

"So let's play," Sarah said, impatiently reaching out for the planchette.

"Wait." Laine held back her sister's hand. "There are rules, like, you're never supposed to play in a graveyard."

"Okay," Iz said, waving her hands at the dining room. "Obviously we're good there."

"Never play alone," Laine went on, trying to

remember everything. "And always end the session with *good bye* or it's bad luck."

"Can we just do this?" Trevor asked, his voice tight with frustration.

Laine nodded and reached in to touch the planchette. One by one, Sarah, Trevor, and Pete all reached in and rested their fingertips on the heart-shaped block of wood.

"I don't even think I believe in these things," Iz said, her hands still in her lap. "But I still don't want to touch it."

"C'mon." Trevor sighed. All he wanted was for this to be over. "They sell 'em in toy stores. It's a game."

Isabelle chewed on her bottom lip for a moment before meeting Laine's pleading eyes. With a sigh of resignation, she reached out and put two fingers on the planchette.

"Circle the board, once for each of us," Laine explained, and the planchette circled the board, five times, clockwise. "And then you say these words: 'As friends we've gathered, hearts are true. Spirits near, we call to you.'"

Laine took a deep breath, looking into the eyes

of her friends. Scared, curious, excited, irritated. As she glanced at the black-and-white photo of Debbie, smiling, next to the board, she realized she didn't know how she felt.

"If there's a presence here," she whispered, "please make yourself known."

Everyone at the table held their breath at the same time.

Nothing happened.

Trevor looked over at Laine, blowing a stray strand of hair from his eyes. Ignoring his silent pleas to give up, she concentrated on the board. There was something in the house—she could feel it.

"Is there a presence among us?" she asked again, counting to ten in her head.

"I feel something," Pete mumbled, eyes locked on the planchette.

"Please." Trevor groaned in disbelief, but still couldn't quite bring himself to move his hands away. "Nothing's happening...."

As he spoke, five pairs of fingers felt the planchette stutter under their touch.

"This is a joke," Sarah said.

"Who is doing this?" Isabelle accused, not so convinced. "C'mon, stop it."

But it didn't stop. Eventually the planchette moved all the way up to the upper left corner of the board, stopping squarely on the word YES.

"Sarah, cut it out," Laine said, half irritated, half excited.

"I'm not pushing it," Sarah yelped, her eyes suddenly wide.

Laine studied her little sister. She'd always thought she could tell when Sarah was lying, but maybe she was rusty. Sarah was the only one who would fake this for kicks; the others just wanted it to be over. Except maybe Pete...

"Is there something you want to tell us?" Laine asked the board, pretending she hadn't even considered that Pete could be capable of such a thing.

"Hello?" he called out when the board didn't respond.

A second later the small piece of wood began to turn under their fingers before sprinting over to the letters H and I.

"'Hi.'" Pete breathed.

The planchette wasn't finished. It moved across the board more quickly this time, sliding over letters, pausing for just a moment on each.

H-I-F-R-E-N-D.

"It's spelling 'Hi, friend,'" Pete said slowly.

"C'mon, Pete." Trevor moved uneasily in his seat. "Stop doing that."

"I'm not doing anything," Pete protested. "It's not me."

"'Hi, friend,'" Laine repeated. Iz looked around the room, fingers trembling against the planchette. Things didn't feel right. "Who is this?"

All five pairs of eyes searched one another, waiting for a response.

"When I was here yesterday, was that you?"

The planchette slid back to the YES spot on the board.

"Who is this?" she asked again, her heart thumping against her ribs. "Please tell us!"

So slowly it was barely moving at all, the lens in the center of the planchette glided over the board, resting on the letter *D*.

"Debbie?" Laine looked over at her sister. Sarah's bottom lip was trembling as she tried to smile back, as she tried to be brave for her big sister.

"I miss you," Laine whispered, her eyes back on the board.

"Me too," Pete added.

Sarah sniffed loudly, a tear escaping. "We all do."

"Okay, okay, if you can hear us, we just wanted to..." Laine's voice trailed off as she searched for the right thing to say. "We just wanted a chance to say good-bye. All of us."

Together they all pushed the planchette to GOOD BYE. Suddenly the lights cut out, leaving them in total darkness. Iz jumped in her seat.

"Oh God." Sarah let out a tiny, terrified moan. She couldn't take it anymore.

"What was that?" Laine turned her head toward the window. "Did anyone else see someone out there?"

"Laine!" Isabelle yelled, her hands still glued to the planchette, as Laine went over to the foyer to investigate. Trevor followed, trying a light switch on the wall. The light was dead.

"It's not even real, okay, Iz?" Sarah said, her

words strong even though tears were running down her face. "It's just a game."

"All of the lights," Trevor said, moving from switch to switch. "They're all out."

Automatically Laine grabbed her cell phone from her pocket and switched on the flashlight app. And the camera.

"I think I hear her," Laine whispered, so as not to scare her away.

"I don't hear anything," Trevor replied.

Laine shushed her boyfriend as she moved through the house, following the sound she was sure she could hear.

"Laine, please stop," he said, following again. "It's not her."

"What if it is?" Laine spun on her heel and stared into his eyes. "What if it is and she has something she needs to tell me?"

Giving up, Trevor let her go, watching as she wandered into the kitchen, searching for something he couldn't see.

"The burner is lit," Laine said, pointing at the stove, scared and triumphant all at once. "Did she do this? Debbie, is that you?"

"Laine, stop!" Trevor tried to catch hold of her arm. "It isn't Debbie."

She turned and shook off his arm, her expression sad and desperate.

The light on the burner went out and the kitchen was silent.

CHAPTER 11

Iz?"

With the Ouija board pressed to her chest, Laine locked the front door of the Garaldis' house as the others hung around on the porch, watching Isabelle walk quickly toward her car.

"Sorry." She held her hands up without turning back. "I just...I can't."

"I think that really freaked her out," Pete said, stating the obvious to his friends. "I gotta be honest, it kinda freaked me out too...."

"Come on." Trevor held out his hand to Laine, ignoring the other guy. "Let's get you home."

Looking back at the house and squeezing the board in her arms, she took it and turned away from Debbie's home.

"Thank you, guys," she said quietly. "For doing this."

Pete and Sarah nodded, Pete with a smile, Sarah with a frown.

"Be honest," Sarah whispered to Pete, slowing her pace so her sister wouldn't hear. "Was it you? Moving the planchette?"

"No," he replied. "You?"

"No." Sarah shook her head emphatically. "No way."

"For all we know it was Laine," he said in a low voice. "Maybe it was something she really needed." The two of them looked over at Laine and Trevor, holding each other in front of the Morrises' car. "Might not have even known she was doing it."

<hr />

Laine's driveway was empty when they got home; their dad was still not home. Sarah clambered out of the car, shutting the door behind her and walking quickly into the house without a word. Wearily Laine pushed her hair out of her face and locked the car door, holding the Ouija board across her chest.

"Why are you bringing that home?" Trevor asked, following her up the steps.

"It was hers. I want it," Laine said, tightening her grip as though he might try to take it from her. "What?"

"Just..." He scratched his chin, light stubble beginning to show through because he hadn't had time to shave that morning. "You really need to believe that it was Debbie?"

She looked up at the stars but they were all hiding behind dark purple strands of cloud. "You were there," she said. "It was weird, right?"

"Yeah, it was weird, but I don't know if that means anything."

"But what if it's her?" she asked. "And this is something she's trying to tell me?"

"You wanted to play and we did." All he wanted to do was grab that board out of her arms and toss it into the garbage can on the curb. "Now we can leave it alone."

Laine glanced down at the board.

"Laine, you said good-bye to her." He stepped a little closer, pushing a loose strand of hair behind her ear so he could see her face. "I know you'll find the moment when you're ready but I think you can start to move on."

She stood there for a moment, looking up into his bright blue eyes, smiling at the pink stripe across his nose where he'd burned himself surfing a couple of weeks ago. All she wanted to do was press her hand against his cheek, kiss him, and tell him he was right. As if he were reading her mind, Trevor pressed his soft lips gently against hers.

"'Night, Laine." He let his lips linger near hers, hoping she was starting to see sense.

"Good night," she said, pulling away and taking the Ouija board inside.

Later that evening, with the whole house resting in peaceful silence, Laine stood before her desk and carefully lit a candle. Her room glowed in the dim golden light as she took her seat and reached her fingers out to the planchette. The Ouija board shone in the candlelight. Laine's eyes rested on the black-and-white picture of Debbie sitting beside the board. She took a deep breath and closed her eyes.

———◆———

The next day every class seemed to last forever and it was tough for Laine to care about conjugating verbs when she was convinced her dead best friend was trying to contact her. After what felt like a lifetime, the final bell sounded and she was free. She stuffed her textbooks in her locker and practically ran out the door. All she wanted to do was get home and figure out what it was Debbie was trying to tell her.

"Hey," Isabelle shouted as she jogged down the steps. "Wait up."

Laine hovered, bouncing from foot to foot. The board would have to wait a little while longer.

"I couldn't sleep last night," Iz said, falling into step with her friend.

"We don't have to talk about it," Laine replied, clearly meaning that she didn't *want* to talk about it.

"Had these weird dreams." Isabelle ignored Laine's curt reply and went right on talking. "Keep thinking about being in that house."

"Iz, I know you didn't want to be there," Laine said in a tense voice. Isabelle went quiet. "You did it for me, I know. So thanks, I owe you."

"Yeah." Isabelle looked away and wiped at her face. Laine gave her a closer look. Was she crying? Even if she wasn't, Iz did not look her best. There were huge dark circles under her eyes and her messy hair was tied in a very un-Isabelle-like topknot.

"Are you mad at me?" Laine asked. She was so caught up in finding out what had happened to Debbie, she kept forgetting that other people were involved in this too.

"I'm not," Iz replied, although Laine was not convinced. "Let's just forget the whole deal, yeah? Last night never happened."

They walked along in silence, Isabelle looking hurt and confused, Laine immediately regretting her snappy attitude. Everyone was on edge, she realized, but lashing out at her friend wasn't going to help.

CHAPTER 12

Nona had taken care of Laine and Sarah until they were far too old to need a babysitter. *Although*, the older woman thought as she picked up a stray white sock in the middle of the hallway, *one could argue that they still do*. Since their dad was working such long hours and their mother showed no signs of ever coming home, she couldn't resist offering to spend some time with her favorite girls, especially after their loss.

Poor Debbie, she thought, spotting another sock at the foot of the stairs. *So young.* Sometimes life did not make any sense. Looking up the stairs, she saw that there was a trail of socks leading all the way to Laine's closed bedroom door.

"Odd," Nona said to herself, collecting them on her way upstairs. Laine wasn't a messy girl; Sarah was the one who didn't know how to clean up her stuff. If anything, Nona would have said Laine was far too responsible for a girl her age. The burden she had taken on when their mother left, and now having to cope with the loss of her best friend, practically another sister. Nona shook her head in dismay.

She opened the door slowly. Nona didn't like invading the girls' privacy, but something seemed off. It was almost as though the stray laundry were leading her to a hiding place under Laine's bed. A bread-crumb trail of sports socks. Huffing a little—her joints were not as young as they used to be—she lifted the dust ruffle on Laine's bed to find a full nest of sports socks. Before she could investigate further, a scraping sound on the desk caught her attention and she turned, just in time to see the planchette Laine had brought back from Debbie's house move across the surface. Climbing up from the floor, Nona picked it up, whispering to herself in Spanish. Breathing in, she glanced down at the board on the desk surrounded by candles and photos of Debbie, and realized what she was holding.

"Por Dios!" She threw the planchette onto the floor and crossed herself, backing out of the room and right into Laine.

"Oh my God," Laine exclaimed, jumping out of her skin. "Nona, what are you—?"

She cut Laine off, pointing at the Ouija board but refusing to look at it. "You should never touch such things," she said, her voice shaky and afraid. "Let alone bring one into your house."

"Nona, it's just a game." Laine heard the words come out of her mouth before she even had time to think about why she was lying. "It was Debbie's."

"You used it, didn't you?" Nona asked, the blood draining from her face. "To contact your friend?"

Laine hesitated, rubbing sweaty palms against her jeans. "Just once."

Nona grabbed the small gold cross at the base of her throat. "To turn to divination is to use something we cannot understand, *Nieta*," she said. "Most of us, our spirits move on when we die, but for some, they remain very close to this world."

Laine shrugged, trying not to give anything away on her face, but Nona knew her too well.

"If one of the living decides to reach out and contact someone on the other side, a connection can be made to that place. But to use such means can be a danger. There are some spirits who weren't ready to die and they are forever seeking a way back into our world."

She took hold of Laine's hand, the soft, cold white hand in her work-toughened warm one. "Promise me, Laine, do not seek answers from the dead. Get rid of that spirit board."

The warning and the request hung heavily in the air. Laine looked into Nona's eyes and saw an urgency she had never seen before. She wasn't playing around, and she wasn't patronizing Laine. She wanted it gone.

"I promise, Nona," Laine said.

Nona breathed out a huge sigh of relief. Laine had never lied to her before. She was a good, smart girl. Nona nodded, kissed her charge on the forehead, and headed out to the stairs. She wanted to finish dinner before Sarah got home and she wanted to be as far away from that Ouija board as possible. Laine watched her old babysitter as she made her way carefully down the stairs, before picking up the planchette and tossing it lightly between her hands. She stared at the smooth piece of wood for a moment, considering Nona's warnings.

Maybe the older woman was right; maybe there were spirits who wanted back into this world...but what if one of those spirits was Debbie?

CHAPTER 13

Trevor frowned, narrowing his eyes on the road ahead as he lowered his chin and powered into the curve. His legs moved around and around, pushing the pedals on his bike, almost as if they were the ones controlling him and not the other way around. When he couldn't get out to the ocean to clear his head among the waves, he liked to put some distance between himself and his problems with his bike. As he forced himself to charge up the last hill on his route, he let go of everything, giving in to the burn of lactic acid in his legs, the trickle of sweat running down his back, and did not stop until he got there.

Finally he sat up on his seat, a small smile of triumph appearing on his face as he exhaled and let himself coast down and around the corner. These last few days had been too much. First Debbie's accident and then the funeral and now all this crazy stuff with Laine. He pulled the bike off the road and grabbed his water bottle, taking a long, steady sip. He had no idea how to try to make things better for her, how to make things right between them. Ever since she'd found out about Debbie, she'd been pushing him away, and now she was all caught up in this damn Ouija board. He tutted to himself, stashing his water bottle back in the holder bolted to the frame of the bike. He knew she was grieving, but he had thought she was smarter than this.

He paused outside a pedestrian tunnel that cut under the road ahead and wiped down his forehead with his shirt, watching as the fluorescent lights inside blinked on and off.

"Maybe it's a message from Debbie," he muttered to himself as he pushed the bike inside.

Trevor did not believe in ghosts. He didn't believe in fairies or spaceships or making wishes either, as much as he wished he did. If there was anything he could do to take this pain away for Laine, he would jump at the chance, but she was so dead set on keeping him at arm's length, to keep going with this ghost crap. And he was certain Pete was encouraging her. The chain on his bike clicked rhythmically as he walked farther into the tunnel, the lights overhead going out one by one before they flashed back into life for just a moment and then flickered back into darkness.

He heard footsteps up ahead and pulled the bike closer to the wall of the tunnel, waiting for someone to pass him, but no one came. He looked over his shoulder at the bright sunshine and considered the tight, stinging sensation on his nose. Sunburned again. Laine was going to kick his ass. Or at least she was if she was still talking to him.

There were the footsteps again.

"Hello?" Trevor called into the darkness, a chill running over his damp back. It was cold inside the tunnel, sheltered from the bold sunlight outside. Cold and dark and weird.

He slowed down, listening for the footsteps again, certain he could see something moving in the shadows at the end of the tunnel, his heart beginning to pound as if he were racing up the hill all over again, when a jogger sprang out of the shadows. Trevor pushed himself against the freezing concrete wall of the tunnel, laughing off the jogger's confused expression. The footsteps faded away as the jogger headed out toward the light, leaving Trevor resting on his handlebars, chuckling to himself. All this dumb ghost stuff was even getting to him now.

He glanced back one more time and the shadows seemed to slide together, covering someone in the darkness.

"Trick of the light," he told himself, pushing his bike a little faster. "That's all."

But as the footsteps padded out into silence, they were replaced by a scratching sound ahead of him. Trevor stopped, listening intently between the clicks made by his bike. The scratching got louder, echoing as he reached the middle of the tunnel, swallowed up in the darkness.

"Hey." He turned around, searching the darkness for the source of the noise. "Somebody there?"

Just another jogger, he told himself as he swallowed hard. Maybe a raccoon or someone's dumb dog. It could be a dog making a scratching sound, right?

"Who is that?" he called. "Pete? I swear to God, dude—"

Before he could finish his sentence, something skittered out of the darkness and stopped dead in front of his feet, making Trevor jump backward and almost trip over his own bike. Gathering himself quickly, he shone the light from his phone down onto the floor. It was a piece of chalk.

Chalk didn't randomly throw itself at people in tunnels, he thought, not unless someone was there to throw it. He picked up the thin white shard and began to power walk toward the exit, toward the sun, when—*BAM*—a shopping cart careened out of the darkness and smashed into the wall right in front of him.

"What the hell?" he shouted, his ears prickling at the sound of footsteps running away. He spun around, shining his tiny torch into the shadows from which the shopping cart had been launched. There was something written on the wall. In chalk.

Long spindly letters spelled out two words. HI FREND.

Just like the message they'd gotten in the game.

No more footsteps, no more scratching, no more flying shopping carts. Trevor stood in the middle of the dark tunnel, staring at the chalk letters, as one by one the overhead lights buzzed back into life, leaving him in the empty tunnel, all alone.

It had been a long day. Isabelle stared at the specials board in the diner, wondering which genius had changed TRY OUR MEATBALLS to TRY OUR BALLZ, YO.

"That's so lovely," she said, rearranging the

letters before the manager saw it. His sense of humor was what Isabelle liked to call "lacking."

"Can you grab the garbage on your way out?" said manager called from the kitchen as she hung up her apron. With a subtle eye-roll she saluted, tied off the trash bag, and continued on her way.

The back of the diner was not a fun place to be, unless you were a raccoon, and even though she might have looked like one with the dark circles under her eyes, Iz was definitely not. Ever since the scene with Laine after school this afternoon, she had wanted nothing more than to go home and sleep. Last night's marathon of bad dreams and an unusually busy dinner service had left her wiped, and now she barely had the strength to toss the garbage into the Dumpster.

The back door of the diner slammed shut with a heavy thumping sound just as she was heaving the gross black bag over her shoulder, reminding her that she was alone. She crossed her arms over her tacky waitress uniform, feeling far too exposed. Summoning a last burst of energy, she sprinted out to the parking lot and fished her car keys from the bottom of her purse. The car flashed its lights and beeped its horn as a hello in the depths of the darkened lot, something white flickering underneath her wipers.

"What is that?" Iz wondered aloud as she sidled up to the car. Her nerves couldn't take any more surprises today. Grabbing the offending article quickly, she realized it was just a piece of paper. "Ooh, furniture sale," she said, balling it up and tossing it into her bag. "Rock and roll."

As she went to open her car door, she noticed odd, condensation-like streaks inside the window. "Great." She sighed. "Just what I need."

She didn't have money to fix the car if something was up but she couldn't get to and from work without it. She stared closely at the marks on the window, trying to figure out where they were coming from. She'd had trouble with her AC before and the seals on her windows were not the best, but these didn't look like regular streaks; they looked like tiny handprints. She was leaning in to take a closer look, her nose almost touching the glass, when a hand appeared from nowhere and slapped the inside of the window, an inch away from her face.

Someone was inside the car.

Iz staggered backward, holding her keys in attack position. She'd known that self-defense class would come in handy. Maybe she couldn't fight back against a Ouija board, but whoever was in that car was about to come in for a whole heap of hurt. As bravely as she could, she grabbed hold of the rear passenger door and flung it open, arm above her head, battle cry in her throat.

There was no one there. Staring at her empty backseat for a moment, she lowered her arms and peered into the front. No one. Pulling open the driver's side door, she looked at the streaks again. What had looked so much like handprints before just looked like regular condensation streaks now. Staring around the empty parking lot, Isabelle let out a small, frightened whimper, got in her car, and turned on the engine. She needed to get home, she needed to sleep, and she needed to pretend this Ouija board stuff had never, ever come her way.

⟡

Pete was at his desk, working on an art project, anything to take his mind off what was happening, when his phone rang. He frowned at the number. Had Iz ever even called him before?

"Hey, Iz," he said, and was cut off by her panicked rambling. "No. No, it doesn't sound crazy at all. Go back inside the diner and I'll pick you up. I'll be there in a few minutes."

He put the phone down and was reaching for his car keys when he saw it. Carved into the desk, right in front of his face.

HI FREND.

CHAPTER
14

You know, before TV and radio, this is how folks would spend their evenings."

A man's voice came out of Laine's phone as she lay on her bed, waiting for Trevor to call to say good night.

"They would light some candles, gather round in the parlor, and attempt to communicate with the spirit world. But in actuality," he went on, "the idea of messages from the board is nothing more than our unconscious minds. It's known as the ideomotor effect. Involuntary motor muscles

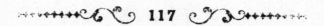

kick in, which drive the movement of the plan-chette. We're simply telling ourselves what we want to believe."

She bit her lip, forcing herself to keep watching and trying to convince herself that she believed him. She stared blankly at Debbie's key ring, sitting on her desk, the little penguin gazing back from behind his sunglasses as the noise began.

"Sarah?" Laine was on her feet and in the hallway before the banging had stopped, but there was nothing to see. It was exactly like the sound in Debbie's house, a long, slow dragging followed by three hard bangs.

"Was that you?" Sarah asked, stepping out of her room, fear in her eyes.

"I thought it was you," Laine replied. Whatever the sound had been, it hadn't come from her sister.

As they stood staring at each other, the sound came again, this time from downstairs. Laine pushed Sarah aside to look. The front door had blown itself open and leaves were rushing inside the house.

"Did you leave that open?" Laine asked. Sarah

shook her head, too afraid to offer a snarky comeback.

"Someone's down there," she whispered. Laine held her arm out as if to protect her, and leaned over the banister.

"Dad?" she called out, treading lightly down the stairs. "Are you home?"

There was no answer. Instead there was a loud scraping sound, as though someone had bumped into a piece of furniture in the dark, and the door slammed shut.

Sarah screamed as Laine bolted back up the stairs and grabbed her sister's hand, pulling her into her room and closing the door quickly behind them. Without thinking, both girls headed into Laine's closet, their favorite hiding spot when they were little girls and Nona was on the warpath.

"Oh my God, oh my God, oh my God." Sarah began to rock back and forth, her breathing hard and heavy.

"Shh." Laine tried to soothe her sister without giving away her own terror as the banging continued downstairs. "Do you have your phone?"

Sarah shook her head, tears beginning to stream silently down her face. The banging noise was getting louder and it was getting closer.

"Shh," Laine said, trying to soothe Sarah with her shaky words. "It's outside. Okay, just be quiet, just be quiet."

Something slammed itself against the closet door. Both sisters gave silent screams, Laine pressing her hand over Sarah's mouth.

The slamming noise came again, rattling the door of the closet. Laine pulled her feet farther underneath herself, holding Sarah as tight as she could as she buried her face in her sister's shoulder. The next slam was even harder, and the door seemed to shake for even longer. Laine grabbed hold of the closet door's handle, holding it tight. Whatever the hell was going on out there, no one was getting into the closet. No one was going to hurt Sarah.

"Laine, make it stop," Sarah whispered into her sister's shirt. "Please make it stop."

BAM BAM BAM BAM BAM.

Whatever was ramming the closet blasted itself against the door over and over and over. It was too much. For a split second the banging stopped and suddenly, whatever was trying to ram the door changed tactics. The door began to rattle and shake. It was trying to get inside. Sarah screamed out, her tears choking her as Laine clung to the door handle for dear life, all her strength pulling down. She had to keep them safe, she had to keep it out. The shaking, the ramming, the slamming noises all began to hit the closet at once, deafening Laine and drowning out Sarah's screams until, all at once, it stopped. The banging noises, the pull on the door handle, all of it. There was nothing but complete and utter silence.

Laine waited until she felt somewhere close to safe and let go of the handle. Nothing happened. A few seconds later she unfurled herself and began to push open the door.

"Don't," Sarah said, grabbing her sister's hand and trying to pull her back into the hiding place.

"Stay right here," Laine replied, trying to sound certain but very aware of the shaking in her voice. She slid out of the closet, pushing the door shut behind her, and felt around for the nearest light switch, finding the lamp by her bed. Her room was entirely undisturbed. Nothing had moved, nothing at all—apart from her laptop. Laine knew she had turned it off but now it was on and open, showing Debbie's online memorial page and telling her she had one new message.

Laine clicked the trackpad to reveal the same words written over and over and over again.

HI FREND HI FREND HI FREND

"What happened?" Sarah asked, but Laine couldn't answer.

Sarah climbed out of the closet and looked around for evidence of what could have caused such a terrifying noise. Instead she found her sister, the blood drained from her face, shaking over her computer. Playing the Ouija board hadn't been an end to all this, she thought to herself; it had just been a beginning.

CHAPTER

15

"Isabelle was shaking when I picked her up," Pete told Trevor, Laine, and Sarah as they walked to school the next morning. Everyone was wired and no one appeared to have gotten any sleep. "I checked on her this morning and she won't even leave her house. And I saw it too, 'Hi friend' carved right into my desk. And when I got home, it was gone."

"Did we all see it?" Laine asked, holding her little sister's hand.

They all turned to Trevor. Reluctantly he nodded a yes and Laine felt her lips tighten into a straight line. "Debbie is trying to reach us," she said, certain this time.

"Let's not go crazy," Trevor said. "We don't know what's happening—"

Before he could finish, Laine stopped him in his tracks with a look.

"Even you said it." Laine jumped to her own defense, sharing Trevor's story for him. "You said it felt like someone was following you. It's got to be Debbie."

"What could she want?" Sarah ran a finger underneath each eye, trying to avoid teary mascara smudges. "Why would she want to scare us like this?"

"If we want to know"—Laine stopped as her friends all turned to look at her—"we're going to have to ask her."

———⋙◆⋘———

Isabelle couldn't say why, but for some reason the Ouija board looked bigger than it had last time, and her friends seemed much farther away.

Reluctantly she reached in to touch the planchette. One by one the others followed suit. Finally, with a purposeful look at Trevor, Pete rested his fingers on the wooden block.

They circled the board clockwise, five times, Laine clearing her throat to say the words.

"I think we should say the words together this time," she said, glancing from Trevor to Pete and back again. As if things weren't tense enough, the air between the two of them bristled with anticipated violence.

"As friends we've gathered, hearts are true," they said together in stilted voices. "Spirits near, we call to you."

Sarah's voice broke on the word *spirits* and Laine threw her a supportive half-smile. This was the only way to end this, she reminded herself.

"If there's a presence here," Laine said aloud, "make yourself known."

Everyone focused on the planchette. For several seconds nothing happened, and then it twitched. Trevor looked over at Pete but the other boy was still staring at the board, his shoulders tight. The planchette shot over to the word YES.

Sarah gasped. Laine looked back to her little sister and, not for the first time, wished she had never dragged her into this.

"Debbie, we're here for you," she called out. "We all got your messages . . . we're here. What do you want to say?"

The planchette twitched and then stopped.

"Debbie." Laine could hear the desperation in her own voice. Why wouldn't Debbie talk to her? No secrets, that was their rule. "Debbie, can you show us a sign?"

The already quiet room grew still, as though all the air were being sucked out at once. Very, very slowly, an empty chair at the table inched backward as though someone were taking a seat.

"We're all seeing this, right?" Sarah asked.

In response the planchette rattled under their fingers and flew off the board onto the table. Laine grabbed it quickly and placed it back in the center of the board as everyone stared at the empty chair. Isabelle shifted slightly in her seat, trying to move away.

"Deb, are you still here?" They all stared at the

chair as Laine spoke. "You didn't kill yourself, did you?"

The planchette pulled five sets of fingers sharply across the board.

NO

"I knew it," Pete whispered, welling up. "I don't know how I even let myself believe—"

"Debbie, if you didn't do this, who did?" Laine interrupted, anxious to get to the truth.

The planchette froze, an odd pulling sensation running through the friends' fingers.

"Did someone hurt you?" Laine asked, insistent this time. "Did someone do something?"

The planchette jerked wildly, resting on YES.

"Oh my God, Debbie." Laine choked up. No matter how much she hadn't wanted to believe that Debbie had killed herself, the thought that someone else had done that to her was almost too much to bear.

"Who did it?" Pete was angry. "Who hurt you?"

The heart-shaped block of wood idled in the middle of the board, almost hesitant.

"Debbie." Sarah broke the painful silence. "We want to help, why won't you answer us?"

Suddenly a calm look came over Pete's face. "I have a question," he said. "Debbie, on our first real date, away from everyone, we told everybody that we went to the fair, but where did we really go?"

He glared at the board, his eyes intense. Laine watched, biting her lip, but nothing happened.

"We went to the lookout." Pete's voice became softer. "By the point, in the canyon. Do you remember that? What I said to you?"

Slowly the planchette inched across the board.

YES

"What I said to you that night, I never told anyone. Do you remember?"

The planchette trembled and circled the word YES once more.

Slowly and with new fear in his eyes, Pete pulled his hands away from the planchette.

"This isn't Debbie," he said in a whisper.

Laine's heart fell into her stomach as she heard his words echo in her head. "What do you mean?"

"I never took her there." Pete looked around at

his friends in earnest. "Not once. Me and Debbie at the lookout? Really?"

Five sets of eyes focused on the board, but Pete's hands stayed in his lap.

"Is this Debbie?" Laine asked. It had to be. It had to be.

The board didn't answer.

"Deb," she whispered, as though it were just the two of them. "Is this you?"

The planchette began to quiver, inching across the Ouija board like an insect. Isabelle let out a gasp as it settled.

NO

"'No,'" Pete said out loud. "Then who the hell is this?"

The planchette began to move in its creepy unnatural way once more, pausing on two letters.

"'DZ'?" Laine said, speaking as it stopped. "Was it you we were talking to the other night?"

It slid over to YES.

"Oh my God." Sarah breathed. "Was this ever Debbie? Were we ever talking to Debbie?"

NO

Laine looked at her sister, suddenly feeling sick.

"Laine." Trevor broke the silence. "We can stop."

She glanced over at him, concern and confusion in his eyes, but she didn't let go of the planchette. Whoever this was, she needed to know.

"When Debbie was playing with the Ouija," she asked, "did she make contact with you?"

Another YES from the planchette.

"DZ, where are you?"

Sarah held her breath, watching as the planchette spelled out another word. "'Here,'" she whispered, sounding grim. "She's in the chair."

Laine stared at the empty seat opposite her, still pulled out from the table. "DZ, are you in the chair?" she asked. But there was no response.

"Maybe that's it?" Trevor suggested. "Maybe it's gone?"

Laine eyed the planchette with determination, remembering what Debbie had told her when they were kids. She picked up the planchette, pulling it away from her friends, and raised it to her face, staring straight at the empty chair in front of her.

"I don't see anything," she said, relieved.

"I think we should get out of here," Sarah said. "This has gone too far."

Laine turned toward her sister, the lens of the planchette still over her eye, but she did not see her sister. She saw something else.

Pale, gaunt, its lips crudely stitched together, it screamed in Laine's face, flesh straining against the stitches.

Laine screamed, dropping the planchette on the board. As it landed, it began to move on its own.

RUNRUNRUNRUNRUNRUNRUNRUNRUNRUNRUN

"'Run'?" Laine translated.

SHE'S COMING

"Who?" Laine screamed, too scared to move. "Who's coming?"

The planchette paused for a moment and then began to move more slowly, almost hovering above the board.

MOTHER

It stopped abruptly, seeming to collapse. Whatever force had been controlling it had let go. Her hands shaking so badly that everyone could see, Laine reached out and picked up the planchette, lifting it to her eye again.

"Don't, Laine," Sarah begged. "Please don't."

But it was too late. Laine stared through the distorted lens, looking around the room until she saw it. The haunting, sewn-up mouth of a frightened-looking little girl, still screaming. And she was pointing at something. Laine whipped around and, for a split second, saw an older figure. A white-faced thing that used to be a woman, pits where her eyes should have been and her mouth opened in an exaggerated scream that no one else could hear. Pointing at Laine, she rushed toward her.

Laine dropped the planchette and screamed, loudly enough for all of them, as something or someone tossed the Ouija board into the air. Everyone ran for the door as it landed back on the table with a crash.

CHAPTER
16

Two minutes later Laine, Sarah, Isabelle, Trevor, and Pete stood on Debbie's front porch.

"What the hell happened in there?" Sarah asked, pulling her sweater tighter around her.

Laine searched for the right words to comfort her sister. "Can we just stop for a second—" she started, but Sarah wasn't about to let her finish.

"No!" she yelled, exploding on her sister. "Debbie played with that board and now she's dead. What if we did the same thing, broke some kind of rule we don't know about—"

Trevor, standing on his own, staring through the darkened window of the house, interrupted. "Just stop talking."

"We did something wrong," Sarah said, turning the full force of her hysterics his way. "And now we're all connected to whatever the hell it is!"

"You going on about it isn't helping anything," Trevor shouted back. "So stop."

Laine took a step toward her sister, trying to comfort her, but Sarah pushed her away. She didn't want to be comforted; she wanted to be away from here, never having played with that damn thing in the first place.

"What do you think now, Trevor?" Pete asked. "Still not a believer in spirits, huh?"

Trevor looked up, something wild taking over his face. Not supernatural but, to Laine, almost as terrifying.

"Shut your mouth," he growled, moving toward Pete until they were face-to-face. "Nobody wants to hear anything from you."

"Don't touch me, dude," Pete said, pulling himself up to his full height.

"It doesn't matter," Laine shouted, watching as

her friends fell apart in front of her eyes. "We're never playing again, okay? We're walking away from the board. The whole thing. And we don't ever come back to this house. Understand?"

Everyone turned to look at her, a mixture of shock and blame and anger on their faces.

"We're finished with this, okay?" She put her arm around Sarah's shoulder and led her down to her car, away from the house, away from her friends, away from it all. "No more."

Neither of the sisters was hungry when they got home, but making dinner was the only thing Laine could think to do. She wanted to feel normal again, just for a moment. Sarah and Laine sat across the table from each other, eating dinner in silence. Laine cut through her chicken, choking the meat down with every bite.

"I saw your college deposit letter," Sarah said. "Why is it in the mail drawer? Don't you need to send that in?"

Laine kept eating for a few moments, as though she hadn't heard her.

"No," she said once Sarah stopped staring at her. "I'm not going."

Sarah set her knife and fork down on her plate. "Seriously? It's all you've talked about for, like, ever."

"It's no big deal," Laine said, taking a sip of water. "I don't need to go right away. There's time."

"It's because of me," Sarah said slowly.

"Let's just eat." Laine did not want to talk about it. Laine didn't want to talk about anything.

"You should go," her sister protested. "You have to go!"

"I don't want to talk about it!" she snapped.

Sarah concentrated hard on her plate. Despite all the makeup on her face, she suddenly looked very young.

"Because I'm gonna get my situation together, Laine," she went on, sounding determined. "Okay? I mean, I was gonna break up with that loser anyway. And skipping school is dumb. I can change."

Laine regarded her sister for a moment. Did she mean it or was she just freaking out after what had happened tonight? *Whatever*, she thought, idly pushing a carrot around her plate, *it doesn't make any difference*. She couldn't leave her dad to cope on his own. She gave Sarah a nod and stuck her fork through the carrot. Sarah tucked into her meal with a small smile on her face but Laine couldn't quite manage the same.

CHAPTER 17

At least Sarah's newfound commitment to her homework would last long enough to give her one peaceful night, Laine thought, sitting at her desk. It had been a whole day since whatever had happened had happened, but every time Laine closed her eyes, she saw that face again. School had felt like torture: Pete, Trevor, and even Sarah spent the entire day avoiding her, and Iz had barely spoken a word.

Laine picked up Debbie's penguin key ring

and spun it around on her finger, wondering, for the millionth time that day, what she could do to make things right. As the keychain came to a rest, swinging slowly back and forth, she noticed a tiny gap between the penguin's head and neck. Laine grabbed the penguin's body and pulled. It was a miniature flash drive. Anxious, she stuck the drive into her computer. What had Debbie saved on here? After the last couple of days, she was hoping for something sweet, a happy memory she might have forgotten, anything that might calm her jangled nerves.

Her screen opened up a new window filled with subfolders, all labeled with random references. Laine's eyes were immediately drawn to one bearing the words LET'S PLAY. She double-clicked it, and the folder opened to reveal dozens of video files. She chose the first one, eyes wide, toes curled around the base of her desk chair, not wanting to touch the floor.

On the screen Laine recognized Debbie's bedroom, the camera focusing in and out on the wall before Debbie jumped into the frame, bandanna over her hair. Laine smiled in spite of herself, her hands in front of her face, laughing as Debbie flexed her nonexistent muscles for the camera.

"Operation Clean House, reporting for duty," Debbie said with a salute.

"Okay, Debbie." Laine recognized Mrs. Garaldi's voice off-camera. "Let's get moving."

Debbie replied by making a face. She grabbed the camera and pointed it up at the ceiling, the entrance to the attic open. "Today's mission," she whispered. "Up there. Ugh."

The screen froze, indicating the end of the clip. Laine smiled to herself. After all the weirdness and upset of the last few days, it felt good to see Debbie happy and messing around. Clicking on the next file, she saw Debbie back in her room, still in the same cleaning clothes but covered in dust and dirt.

"House scrubbed," she said, tired but with a glint in her eyes. "We're talking every nook and cranny. I'm not gonna lie to you, it sucked bigtime but I found something. Check this out."

Debbie moved out of frame and reappeared holding the Ouija board.

Laine froze.

"It's cool, right?" Debbie went on, displaying the board like a game show hostess. "And this." She held out the wooden planchette. "They go together!"

Laine realized her hand was shaking as she reached for the mouse to open the next video. "She found it in her house?" she whispered. "She didn't buy it, she found it."

"Do I like my find?" Debbie asked in a mock spooky voice, visibly pushing the planchette around the board herself. "Yes. Am I cleaning the attic again? No. What do you know, it works!"

The next video had been shot at night. Debbie was in her room with just her bedside lamp lighting the scene. Laid out on the floor in front of her was the Ouija board.

"There's something you're supposed to say first," Debbie said, as much to herself as to the camera. "Oh yeah, as friends we've gathered, hearts are true, spirits near, we call to you."

She paused to throw a quick grin at the camera. Laine began to feel nauseous.

"Is there a presence here?" Debbie asked, her fingers resting on the little block of wood. With a quirked eyebrow, she gave the camera a look. And then the planchette began to twitch under her hands. She inched backward as it slid over to the word YES.

"Okay, that didn't just happen."

She stared at the board for a long moment before shifting her gaze to the camera. After a couple of seconds, she pulled her hand away from the planchette and switched off the video.

The sick feeling growing in her stomach, Laine opened the next clip, wishing there were something she could do to stop this, but it was like watching a horror movie someone had spoiled—she already knew how this ended. The clip filled her computer screen, set up the same as the last one. Debbie's room, nighttime. The camera zoomed in and out a little as Debbie settled herself in the frame.

"Something weird happened last night," she told the camera, considerably less carefree than she had been the night before. She stared right into the camera, right into Laine's eyes. "So I'm doing a little test. I need to make sure I'm not losing it."

Slowly she placed her fingertips back onto the planchette and circled the board once.

"Never play alone," Laine whispered, turning up the volume on her computer and resting her own fingertips on her mouse.

"Wanted to see if you were out there again," Debbie said to the board, closing her eyes and concentrating. Without Laine's touching anything, the footage on the screen fast-forwarded for a few seconds before pausing and skipping back. The planchette on the screen began to move quickly, resting on certain letters, spelling its message for Debbie.

"*F-R-E-N-D?*" Debbie stared at the board, amazed. "You mean 'Friend'? 'Hi, friend'?"

Laine's face fell. Whoever it was, it was not Debbie's friend.

CHAPTER 18

Isabelle hadn't been scheduled to work a double shift at the diner, but after the incident at Debbie's house, she'd thought she wanted to be busy. Staring at her reflection in the bathroom mirror, she promised herself she would never think anything so dumb again. Ten hours later all she wanted to do was curl up in her bed, close her eyes, and pretend everything was okay.

She pulled her hair into a ponytail on top of her head, completely exhausted, and turned on the faucet to run a hot, steamy bath. There was nothing comforting about the smell of fried food, she thought, sniffing the end of her ponytail and wrinkling her nose. While the bath filled, she reached inside the medicine cabinet for her floss. Just because she had connected to the dead with a spirit board didn't mean dental hygiene wasn't important. Absently pulling the floss back and forth between her teeth, Iz let her mind wander. Her history report was due and she had a date on Saturday—these were the things she should be worried about, she told herself.

Suddenly her hands stopped moving, as though the floss were stuck on something. Looking up into mirror, her reflection obscured by steam, Iz saw it and tried to scream.

HI FREND

She tore at the floss but it wouldn't budge as it stitched her lips into silence. As she struggled with herself, an unseen force flew at her, almost knocking her off her feet. Steadying herself with one hand on the vanity unit, Iz turned, panicked, but saw nothing. Whipping back around, she stared at herself in the now-clear mirror. Her lips were completely fused together. Slowly her eyes rolled back in her head, the deep brown turning white, and then she was calm.

Iz looked over at the hair dryer, plug carefully coiled around the handle, and picked it up, methodically unwinding the cord. Slowly she plugged it in. Turning off the taps, she tested the water of the bath with her hand and smiled against the stitches in her mouth. She stepped into the tub, luxuriating in every second as the warm water enveloped her body. And then she reached out for the hair dryer, turned it on, and dropped it into the water.

CHAPTER 19

You've been through a lot the last few weeks." A matronly-looking counselor sat across the desk from Laine, vague concern in her eyes, a list of bullet points on the card in front of her. "An awful lot. First with Debbie and now Isabelle."

Laine looked away. She didn't want to discuss this with a stranger. She didn't want to talk about it with anyone—her dad, Nona, none of them could help her.

"I wanted to talk to you because, well." The

counselor shuffled her cards, looking for her next cue. "Things like this can happen in a cluster. In a group of friends, when you lose someone close to you, it can make you think things."

Laine raised an eyebrow.

"Dark things," the counselor expanded. "And sometimes...I just want to make sure you know you can talk to me. If you're thinking any dark things."

She cleared her throat and pushed a pile of pamphlets across the desk.

"There's a lot of very, very helpful information in there about...suicide," she said, lowering her voice on the last word. She really wasn't very good at this, Laine thought. "And about how to process the—"

"You don't have any idea what you're talking about," Laine cut her off, crossing her arms over her chest, looking away.

The counselor blinked. "I'm sorry?"

"Debbie, Isabelle?" Laine leaned forward, knowing how crazy she was about to sound. "Look, I know you've got to go through the playbook here but I know—*I know*—they didn't do this to themselves. And I've got to stop it."

She stood up, grabbing her book bag.

"Laine, we only want to help you," the counselor said, her cheeks flushed. "Please."

"You can't," Laine said sadly. "I'm not even sure who can."

She walked through the hallway, moving quickly past Debbie's and Isabelle's lockers, refusing to look at all the flowers and pictures and tearful so-called friends hanging around. Over by his locker, Trevor saw her coming and turned away, looking for a way out. She noticed Pete, sliding books into his locker opposite. He looked away. He didn't want to get involved.

"Trevor," she called, breaking into a jog and laying a hand on his shoulder to stop him from running. "Trevor, please. We need to talk. All of us."

"You made us play," he said quietly. "And now Isabelle's dead."

"I know," Laine said, the shock of his words, his tone of voice, hitting her like cold water. "And I'll never forgive myself."

Trevor took a step closer to her, his voice nothing but a desperate whisper. "It's coming for all of us, you know that? So who's next?"

Laine stared at him, his hand so tight around her arm it almost hurt. He had never, ever hurt her. Paralyzed with fear, she watched as Trevor turned and walked away. Once he was gone, her legs began to shake. Too afraid of what might happen if she stood still, Laine held her bag tightly to her chest and ran out the front doors, into the sunlight.

"Hey," she said, as Pete took a seat beside her outside the school gates. "Look, back there with Trevor—"

Pete shook his head. "He's right," he said. "Two people are already dead."

"I need you," Laine said in a clear, plaintive voice. She wasn't used to asking for help. Ever since her mom disappeared, Laine had been keeping things going. Taking care of Sarah, looking after her dad, working her ass off in school to keep her grades up. But this was altogether too much for one person to handle. "It's just us now."

"What does this spirit want to do with us?" Pete asked, staring at his shoes. "Why is it doing this to us?"

"It's angry?" Laine reasoned. It didn't seem beyond the realm of possibility. "When Debbie played, she woke something up in that house."

They sat together in the sunshine, feeling nothing but the cold realization that whatever had been disturbed would not go quietly.

"Pete," Laine said. "Please, I need your help."

He looked at Debbie's best friend for a moment and nodded.

Laine gave him as brave a look as she could muster.

CHAPTER 20

Without a word Laine opened the door to the Garaldis' dark house, her face glowering with grim determination. She turned to look at Pete and started up the stairs without even looking around. He sighed and followed, reaching for the handrail. Laine focused on the stairs in front of her rather than all the photos of Debbie on the walls; it was still too hard to think about what had happened right where they were standing. At the top of the stairs, she opened her friend's bedroom door, hoping this would be the last time.

Downstairs in the dining room, the Ouija board sat on the dining room table where she left it, completely still, waiting for them.

Laine turned on a flashlight and shone it up at Debbie's ceiling. This was the entrance to the attic. This was what she had seen in Debbie's video clips.

"I think that's where she found it," she whispered to Pete. He grabbed the chair from in front of the desk and put one foot on the seat.

"I'll go," he said. Laine had already suffered so much, he wanted to do this.

"No," Laine said, pushing him gently out of the way. "I need to do this. Let me. Please?"

Pete looked her in the eye, finding only utter certainty. If she was afraid, he couldn't tell. Clearly she meant what she said. She pulled the short ladder down from the attic door. Stepping back, he helped her onto the ladder and hoisted her up into the attic, saying every prayer he knew that she would come back down again.

The attic was dark and dusty, not that she hadn't been expecting it to be, but a certain shiver came over Laine as she began to paw her way across the floor.

"You got it?" Pete called from the bedroom. Even though he was only a few feet below her, he sounded very far away.

"I'm good," she replied. A lie.

"What's up there?" he called again, hoping that if he kept talking to her, he could keep her safe. Laine switched the flashlight to its full beam, trying to get a sense of her surroundings. The attic was big but the roof sloped so low, she couldn't really stand up anywhere. Crouching down, she spotted some boxes resting against the wall, right in the narrowest part of the attic. Debbie hadn't been kidding about clearing out; there was next to nothing else in there.

"I'm going farther in," she shouted down to Pete. "There're some boxes up here."

Pete stood below the entrance to the attic, just barely able to hear Laine's voice. It was strange standing in Debbie's bedroom without her there. If he tried, not that hard, he could see her on her bed, laughing, smiling. One of her theater masks, some dumb thing he'd bought for her at a carnival, hung on a nearby wall. He pulled it from its hook, holding it against his face the way he had the first time they saw it.

"Debbie," he whispered, turning it over in his hands. Why hadn't he realized something was wrong? Instead, he had felt sorry for himself, sure that she wanted to break up. He should have known that people went through tough times and couldn't always ask for help. "I'm so sorry."

Outside, in the hallway, he heard a creaking sound. Or had it come from the attic? Setting the mask down on the desk, he opened Debbie's bedroom door.

Up in the attic Laine reached the boxes. Blowing cobwebs out of her face, she opened them up, resting the flashlight between her knees. Some old records, an ancient Monopoly board. *Why couldn't Debbie have played with that instead?* she wondered. At the very bottom was a stash of black-and-white photos. Laine pulled them out, flipping through the pile, the same faces peering back at her time and time again. It was a family—a father, a mother, and a teenage son. He looked about Sarah's age, she thought. There they were, the three of them smiling and laughing at the beach, beside a Christmas tree, and then on the front porch of a house that was instantly familiar.

Debbie's house.

Laine flipped feverishly to the next picture and her breath caught in her throat. It was the mother and a pretty young daughter, sitting in front of the Ouija board with their fingers resting on the planchette. Nothing more than a family game. Only there was something wrong with the photos. Someone had been cut out on the other side of the mother. Laine went back to look at the other photos. Every one was the same. Every one had been cut.

"Something happened in this house," she whispered, looking through more and more hacked-up photographs.

Pete looked out into the hallway. Nothing. No creaking, no dragging, no banging. Heading back into the bedroom, he closed the door behind him before he noticed that the theater mask had moved.

"Laine?" he called up into the attic, suddenly nervous.

But Laine couldn't hear. With the photos in a stack behind her, she reached over to grab a pile of rags that rested beside the box. Only it wasn't a pile of rags. It was a very old, very grubby doll. Laine held it up to get a better look; nothing but a doll.

Pete paced up and down underneath the entrance to the attic, waiting to hear Laine's voice, completely oblivious to the shadowy figure that was watching him from the other side of Debbie's bed. When he turned his back, staring up into the darkness of the attic, it picked up Debbie's theater mask, tilting its head and regarding the boy across the room.

A sudden feeling of being watched washed over him and Pete turned suddenly, catching sight of something in the mirror. But there was no one. Just the theater mask on the floor.

"Laine?" he called. "Laine, we gotta go!"

"I'm coming," Laine replied, putting the creepy doll back where she'd found it.

"Are you all right?" he asked, his gaze flicking

from the empty bedroom into the abyss of the attic. For what felt like forever, there was no reply. Pete could feel his heart rate mounting. Something was in the room, something was watching him, something was—

"Here." Laine reached a hand down out of the ceiling. "Grab this, it's heavy."

She handed him a big box of photos, her flashlight rolling away toward the back corner of the attic. Laine watched as it came to a sudden stop. The beam of light fell on the face of the doll.

"That's not where I left it," she said.

And the doll wasn't how she had left it. The perfectly normal face was now gruesomely deformed, the mouth stitched together with erratic black stitches.

Laine gasped, breathing in too much dust and coughing madly as she tried to climb back down the ladder.

"Are you okay?" Pete asked as she fell from the ceiling, collapsing in a pile on top of her friend, staring back up at the attic, waiting for something to follow.

CHAPTER 21

"This is the family."

Back at her house, Laine, somewhat composed, showed Pete the photographs she had found in the attic. She hadn't spoken the whole car ride over but now that she was showered and changed, she needed to show him what she had discovered. "It's Debbie's house, right?"

"Right," Pete agreed. "From the look of it, I'd say it's the late forties, maybe the early fifties?"

"Is there any way to look up the records?" Laine

asked, not really knowing what she wanted. "Are there property archives or anything?"

"We can try," Pete said with a shrug, still leafing through the photos. "Weird, look at this one." He held up a photograph patched together with a piece of tape. "It's like there's part of the photo missing. Like they ripped something out and taped it back together."

Laine grabbed the photo of the mother and daughter playing at the Ouija board and realized it had been cropped too. "It's all of them," she said. "Someone's been cut out of all of them. But who would do that?"

Pete placed the taped photo carefully on the table, eyes on Laine.

"And more importantly," he said, nervous energy all around him, "why?"

<hr />

Laine sat in front of her computer long after Pete had left, scrolling through newspaper archives, looking for answers. Her tired eyes scanned every page, seeing nothing.

"Wait," she whispered, scrolling back up. "Is that...?"

A faded image on the screen showed a house that looked just like Debbie's. Laine enlarged the image. It *was* Debbie's house. Only it wasn't Debbie standing outside; instead there were two young girls, dressed in their Sunday best, one smiling for the camera, the other looking so sad.

"'Doris and Paula Zander,'" Laine read aloud.

"What?" Sarah appeared in the open door. "What are you doing?"

Laine turned toward her sister. "Sarah, come look at this," she said. "DZ had a sister. A twin."

She entered the names into a search engine, and her eyes widened as dozens of news stories appeared. The first one showed the same picture of the twins, next to another photo of a tall, slender woman with huge, dark eyes. Laine recognized her immediately. Mother.

"What?" Sarah said, leaning over her sister's shoulder.

"DZ was a missing girl, Doris Zander," Laine

said, reading. "She lived in Debbie's house but they never found her. Never found a body."

"So?" Sarah looked confused. "That's why she's doing this?"

"If she's still in that house somewhere, it means Debbie played the game in a graveyard." She winced, looking at the picture of little DZ.

"And alone," Sarah said.

"But we also know who was cut out of all of those pictures I found," Laine continued. "Paula Zander."

"Why would you cut out the kid who survived?" Sarah asked. "None of this makes any sense."

"Oh my God." Laine breathed, flipping over to the next article. "Maybe this is why."

She reached out for Sarah's hand as she read the next article. A grainy photo of Paula, smiling so wide, next to the headline "Girl, 10, Murders Mother."

CHAPTER 22

A tall, tired-looking man in a gray uniform held the door open for Laine, a look of disapproval on his face. He nodded curtly as she entered, and closed the door behind her. Laine heard the lock turn and swallowed hard.

"They said my niece was here to visit."

A tall, dignified-looking elderly woman sat on a hospital bed, eyeing Laine with suspicion. She motioned for her to come over. Slowly Laine moved toward the bed and sat on the edge.

"I don't have a niece."

"My name is Laine. Laine Morris," she said, glancing at the bars on the window and looking away quickly.

"Should that name mean something?" Paula Zander asked.

"No," Laine replied. "You wouldn't know me. I'm here to ask about your sister, Doris."

Paula sat up a little straighter, surprise on her face, followed by a bittersweet smile.

"Doris." She closed her eyes and the smile grew wider.

"I'm sorry," Laine said, not wanting to interrupt her reverie. "I don't mean to be insensitive."

"No, no." Paula opened her eyes again and offered Laine a warm smile. "Too many years have passed for that. A lot of years."

Laine relaxed a little, pleased to see that the memory of her sister didn't upset her. Now Laine could ask the questions she had to ask.

"My best friend, Debbie, lived in your old house," she started. Paula perked up again. "She's . . . she's not alive anymore."

Paula's smile faded and she nodded slowly.

"And I know this is going to sound crazy," Laine went on, "but I think I know why. I believe there's a presence in that house."

She stopped, waiting for Paula to laugh or throw her out or something. *And she's the one in the mental hospital*, Laine thought.

"Oh." Instead Paula knitted her hands together and sighed. "I wouldn't be surprised if there were more than one."

Laine sat up, shocked, and stared at the old woman. She looked back with kind eyes.

"Doris, DZ," she said. "Is that what you called her? And your mother?"

"My mother..." Paula said slowly, her eyes darkening.

"From the pictures—"

"Photos?" Paula snapped to attention. "You have my family photos?"

"I do," Laine said, inching toward her. "I can bring them to you. Or send them, if you like?"

"Oh, please bring them," she begged. "I haven't seen my sister's face in a long time. At least, not her real face."

"I believe I saw her," Laine said, hoping no one

was listening in. If the staff could hear this conversation, they might not let her leave. "Me and my friends. Her lips were... They were... "

Paula closed her eyes once more, a deep sadness washing over her that Laine could feel as well as see. "Mother did that to her," she whispered.

Laine nodded, holding her breath as she waited for Paula to speak.

"My mother practiced mediumship." Her voice was ragged with age at the edges but bore no trace of confusion or doubt. Laine listened intently. "And if practice makes perfect, let me tell you, she was pretty damn good. Depending on your point of view. She'd conduct séances, use the spirit boards, anything. A bit reckless, actually."

She leaned in toward her young visitor.

"And Doris, well, Doris loved Mother. Wanted to help her. Was fascinated by it all. And when Momma's séances got bigger, started to really make connections, she needed a vessel. A vessel to give them a voice."

Laine looked puzzled. "Who?"

"The spirits," Paula replied. "She used Doris. An innocent vessel, an open door." Paula regarded

Laine carefully. "But something went wrong, something with Mother. All that time chasing the dead, living in all those shadows. Something snapped and she couldn't turn it off. Couldn't break the connection."

Laine knew what was coming next. She felt herself tearing up before Paula even said the words.

"All that evil, all those voices. Mother became consumed by them. She was insane. So she did that, to Doris. To her lips. To stop the spirits talking through her anymore. And then Doris went missing."

It was horrifying. Laine thought of her own missing mom, how her heart ached every day that she was gone, with no idea where she was or why she didn't love her family enough to stay, but the idea of a mother becoming such a monster? Totally inconceivable.

"She never left the house, did she?" Laine asked.

"No, she didn't," Paula replied simply. "Mother was consumed by evil. She wasn't my mother anymore and she...she killed her. She killed Doris. After that, I did what I had to do, to stop her. And that's why I'm here. Doesn't mean she's gone, though." She eyed the bars on her window wistfully and then looked sharply back at Laine. "How did you see her?"

Laine blinked, lost in the story. "What?"

"You said you saw Doris," she repeated, her eyes widening as she spoke. "Her lips. How did you see her? She wouldn't be able to be seen, not unless... What did you do in the house?"

"Look, I just need to know how to stop whatever is happening," Laine said, reaching out and taking Paula's hand. "My friends are dying."

"You opened up a channel," Paula said, narrowing her eyes at Laine. "Made a connection, with what? Hmm, a spirit board, I'll bet."

Laine nodded, full of remorse. "Yes."

"And now... she's awake again?"

Another nod. "Both of them," Laine said. "Mother too."

Paula's smile faded fast. "If you could see them..."

"Only through the planchette," Laine said quickly. "Only then."

"Not for long," Paula corrected. "They're getting stronger. The points of connection. In your case, the board and the body, the link between them and the energy grows. It's hard to stop."

Laine grew scared again. These were not the answers she had been looking for.

"If you want this to stop, you're going to have to listen to me very, very carefully." Paula squeezed her hand hard. "Because, you poor girl, this is going to be incredibly dangerous."

CHAPTER
23

Laine and Sarah walked up to Debbie's house wordlessly. Laine leaned against the gate, willing her legs not to collapse underneath her. Only she had seen what had happened to Doris, and only she had seen Mother. Only she had sat, terrified, and listened to Paula's instructions for how to end this once and for all.

"Mother used to have a secret room," Paula had told her. "She sealed it up, after Doris, down in the basement."

She glanced over to see Pete and Trevor approaching the house from opposite ends of the street, the same look of dark acceptance on their faces.

"Don't go at night," Paula had warned. "And don't go alone. Mother will try to stop you."

"I got your text," Trevor said. "Gotta say, I'd have preferred to meet at the diner."

"Yeah, well, we can't solve our problem at the diner," she replied, Paula's warning ringing through her head.

Together they walked up to the door. Laine opened it quickly, purposefully striding right past the dining room and the board, heading straight for the furnace.

"It's supposed to be here somewhere," she said, feeling the wall, looking for a hidden doorway. "Paula said it would be here."

"This is crazy, Laine," Trevor said while Pete and Sarah hovered behind him. "We should just leave it alone. We shouldn't be here."

She turned, ready for an argument, and instead felt a look of horror take over her face.

Trevor saw the look in her eyes and panicked. "What?"

Laine pointed. "The shadows."

Right there on the wall, beside Trevor's shadow, was that of a second person. The shadow of a tall, thin woman. But there was no one else there, just Laine, Trevor, Sarah, and Pete.

"What the..." The strange shadow rushed along the wall at Trevor's and suddenly he was knocked over and dragged down the corridor, yelling out for help as he went.

"Trevor!" Laine screamed.

"I'll get him," Pete promised, running down the hall, chasing Trevor and his new shadow. As he passed through the door, it slammed shut behind him.

"Trevor!" Laine stared at the door for a moment before turning her attention to the wall in front of her. Mother was trying to scare her, trying to keep her out of her secret room. "Help me," she yelled at Sarah. "We have to get in here."

As the sisters pulled the wallpaper away, a vent became visible.

"Stay here," Laine instructed her sister as she opened it up. The boys began hammering on the door, demanding to be let back in, but Laine shook her head at Sarah. "Not until I know it's safe."

Sarah nodded, tearfully embracing her big sister and then scuttling away, her back pressed against the wall, as Laine crawled into the hidden passage.

It was dark inside, but not just from the lack of natural light. The walls had been painted black, every surface as dark as night, lit only by Laine's flashlight.

"Are you okay?" Sarah called through the vent. "Laine?"

"I'm okay," she replied, turning the flashlight onto an altar running the length of the room. "Stay there, I think I've found her."

As she followed the altar, she began to see all kinds of mystical paraphernalia placed haphazardly around the room. Candles, crystals, runes, voodoo dolls. It all made her skin crawl. As she reached the end, she came across a sheet covering something and weighted down with more candles, more crystals. Laine reached out to pull back the sheet with a shaky hand, afraid of what she might find underneath.

"Laine?" Sarah called.

"I found her," Laine replied softly. She moved the sheet back carefully, revealing the mummified remains of Doris Zander. "Oh my God."

The body was covered in talismans, crystals, and rune-inscribed trinkets. The parting gifts of a madwoman, trying to control spirits by torturing a little girl. Laine could see that Doris had been beautiful once, but now all that was left was gray, waxy skin, half of her face obscured by an ugly leather muzzle. As Laine bent over the body to take a closer look, her flashlight began to flicker.

"Not now," she muttered. "Please no."

She hit it a couple of times but that didn't help. As it sputtered in and out, Laine noticed a pack of matches beside the candles around Doris's body. She grabbed them quickly, lighting as many candles as she could before the flashlight died completely.

Once the candles settled into a dim glow, Laine steeled herself to return to the task at hand. Paula had told her what to expect, what she had to do, but now that she was there, in the middle of it all, everything felt so overwhelming. She reached across Doris's face to unfasten the muzzle, pulling away the decaying leather to reveal the crudely stitched-together mouth.

"What kind of monster..." she whispered, tears rolling down her cheeks as she pulled the wire cutters out of her bag and began to snip away at the stitches, her heart breaking with every cut. Laine felt so alone. She needed to hear her sister's voice. "Sarah?"

But there was no reply. A wash of terror rushed over her as she looked back through the crawl space and saw nothing. Terrified of what could have happened to her baby sister, she pressed on with the job, freeing Paula's sister from her eternal torment as she had promised. Only she wasn't fast enough.

"NO."

Mother appeared, illuminated by the candles. She wasn't a shadow and Laine didn't need the planchette to see her this time. Paula had been right, the ghosts were getting stronger. She reached out with deathly thin fingers to grasp at Laine, at the wire cutters.

"Get away from her!" The ghost's voice was low and raspy as she charged toward Laine. Two stitches left, Laine told herself, trying to control her hands and finish the job before Mother could reach her. One stitch.

"No!" the ghost of Mother screamed, a cold, painful noise that tore at Laine's eardrums. She dropped the wire cutters and covered her ears, wincing in pain.

Without warning Doris's ghost burst forth from the mummified body as her jaw dropped, open for the first time in so long. Laine cowered in the corner as she began to wail; it was so much louder, so much more intense than the roar of the mother. Doris's ghost rushed toward that of her mother and let out a soul-shattering scream. The tall, thin woman faltered backward for a moment before blasting apart against the force of Doris's scream. Every candle in the room went out.

Laine fumbled in the darkness, finally finding

her flashlight by Doris's resting place. It turned on. She looked down at the body of the little girl, her jaw hanging slack, finally free. Doris, Debbie, Isabelle. It was finally over.

Stepping backward toward the crawl space, Laine began to cry.

———————✥———————

Laine pulled open the shades in the Garaldis' living room for the first time since Debbie had died and sunshine rolled through the house. Sarah, Trevor, and Pete sat on the couches, bruised and battered but alive.

"It feels different somehow," Pete said, looking at the walls, waiting for an explanation. "It feels changed."

"Yeah," Laine said, smiling. She looked over at the gallery of family photos along the staircase, her eyes filling with tears for her best friend. At least she could be at peace now. "Yeah, it does."

It does feel different, she thought to herself. *It feels over.*

CHAPTER 24

Pete was restless when he got home. He tried reading, studying, even watching a movie, but nothing helped. His eyes kept drifting over to the picture of him and Debbie that sat in a silver frame on his desk next to his paintbrushes, pencils, and X-ACTO knife. He was relieved that the nightmare was over but he still couldn't seem to forgive himself for letting Debbie slip through his fingers. Sure, they'd stopped DZ, but why hadn't he been able to help Debbie when he knew something was wrong? Instead he'd been selfish, worrying that she wanted to break up with him instead of actually trying to get to the bottom of what was the matter.

He kicked off his shoes and threw himself back on his bed, turning his head to stare at himself in the mirror on his closet. Only he wasn't alone.

"Debbie?"

Pete blinked, rubbing his eyes, but she was still there. In the mirror he saw Debbie holding the framed photo, her head hanging down sadly. She turned, her back to him, to replace the frame. He leaped up to touch her but when his fingers reached the mirror, she was gone. Panting, Pete stared at his own wild expression, not sure whether he could trust what he was seeing. He closed his eyes. It couldn't be.

When he opened them, there was a new figure in the mirror.

It was Doris Zander.

Pete pressed himself against the mirror, staring at her wide-open mouth, with nowhere to run. A torrent of screams rushed out of her, a thousand voices instead of one. Pete bent over, collapsing in pain, his ears bleeding from the sound.

Then it stopped.

Doris was gone, the room was silent, and Pete straightened up slowly.

Calmly he turned toward the mirror as his eyes rolled back, completely white. Utterly passive, he took a seat at his desk and methodically rolled up his shirt sleeve before reaching into his pencil cup. With one last look at the framed picture of Debbie, he pulled out the X-ACTO knife.

Click. Small blade.

Click click. Medium blade.

Click click click. Long blade.

———⋆⊱✦⊰⋆———

Ahh, my tenacious niece." Paula Zander smiled beatifically at Laine as she was walked into the visitors' room at the hospital by another armed guard. "It's good to see you again."

"My friends are still dying!" Laine cried out as soon as the guard was gone.

Paula wore a look of confusion. "What?"

"I did everything you said!" Laine half spoke, half sobbed. "We found the body, I cut the stitching, and she sent Mother away, just like you said. But it didn't work. Why didn't it work?"

She rubbed a hand over her face, smearing tears against her cheek as Paula's face slipped into a mask of nothing. Laine couldn't stop thinking about Pete, the way his parents had found him. All that blood.

"Mother must have come back," she reasoned. "Because my friend Pete, another friend of mine, he's dead. It's not over."

Across from her, Paula remained unmoved.

"She's free," she said, almost casually. The corners of her mouth began to curl and she covered her face with her hands, her shoulders shaking. Laine didn't know what to do, how to console her. And then she realized Paula wasn't crying. She was laughing.

"You lied to me," Laine said in cold realization.

Paula nodded, laughing maniacally. "Free," she repeated. "She's free."

"Your mother didn't hurt us when we were there," Laine said, piecing together the events of the last few days. "She never tried to hurt me, just stop me. It wasn't your mother who was evil, was it? It was..."

"Free, she's finally free!" Paula said again. "I told her! I always told her I would help her when I could."

She leaned in toward Laine, as though she were about to tell her a precious secret. "I heard the voices too, you know," she whispered, her eyes dancing. "They tell you the most wonderful, awful things."

Laine stood up quickly, knocking her chair over in her rush to get away from the mad old woman.

"You'll hear them, little girl," Paula promised, rocking back and forth in her chair. "You'll hear them soon enough because she'll come for you too. She'll be nice to me now, she'll keep her promise!"

The old woman doubled over, hysterical screams echoing through the hospital's halls as Laine ran away, as fast as she could.

CHAPTER 25

Nona didn't know what to do. She sat on the couch, listening to Laine tell the story as Sarah whimpered at her side.

"You have to break the connection," she said eventually. "Or the old lady is correct, it will keep coming for you."

"I'll burn the board," Laine said, resolutely. "I'll do it right now."

"That won't be enough," Nona said, fingering her necklace. "A spirit this strong will come back. A connection to a spirit, once it is made, is difficult to break. The board is just the conduit; you have to sever the connection on both sides."

"How?" Sarah asked. "How do we do it?"

"Your connection is through the board and through that little girl's body," Nona explained. "The spirit lives through both of them, so you must destroy them both."

"Destroy the body?" Laine thought back to the mummified little girl and felt sick to her stomach.

"And the board." Nona nodded. "And you must hurry. I will not lose either of you, *Nieta*, you must do it now."

<hr />

*R*eluctant was not a strong enough word for the way Trevor felt when he pulled his bike to a halt outside Debbie's house. He looked around for Laine's car but couldn't see it.

"First here," he mumbled, staring at the building as though it had the answers he needed. Out of the corner of his eye, he saw a flash of blonde hair disappear around the back of the house.

"Hey, Laine," he called, resting his bike against the fence. "Wait up!"

"Trevor," she shouted back. "Come quick, it's by the pool!"

As much as he didn't want to be there, he couldn't let her go into that house alone. Whatever had happened, whatever was going to happen, he loved Laine. If there was anything he could do to spare her any more misery, he would do it.

"Laine?" he rounded the back of the house but saw no one, and there was nothing by the pool. He walked closer to the water. Someone had pulled the cover back halfway and the surface was covered in leaves. In the far corner he saw some movement, as if something had fallen in.

"No way," he said out loud, walking away. "Not my problem."

Turning toward the house, Trevor headed over to the back stairs and right into the screaming face of Doris Zander. He flew back, knocked over by the strength of a thousand spirits, all echoing through her tiny, used-up body and crashing into him, throwing him into the pool. He struggled against the screaming, thrashing around to get a grip on the cover, to pull himself out of the water, but something seemed to grab hold of his body and pulled Trevor deep under the water.

The surface rippled for a few moments, the calm concentric circles smoothing out the aqua-blue water, before everything was still.

<hr />

Trevor?" Laine called out as she and Sarah entered the house. "It's us."

"Where is he?" Sarah asked, clutching her sister's arm. Trevor's bike was outside the house, but he was nowhere to be seen.

"Trevor!" Laine yelled. No point worrying about waking any spirits now. All she wanted was to see his face. They moved through the dark house, Laine's not-so-trusty flashlight illuminating their way. She stopped short in the kitchen, pushing Sarah behind her. There was someone in there.

"Trevor?" she said warily.

It was her boyfriend, standing in the kitchen with his back to her, but something was wrong. Laine stepped a little closer and noticed a pool of water around his feet. He was dripping. She stretched out her hand to touch his shoulder and when he spun around to face her, Laine wished with all her heart that he hadn't. His mouth was stitched shut and his eyes were white. Trevor screamed against DZ's handiwork before bursting into a cloud of black smoke. Gone. Forever.

"She already got him," Laine whispered. The floor where Trevor's ghost had stood was completely dry. He had never been there.

"What do we do?" Sarah asked in her tiniest voice.

"Get the board," Laine ordered.

CHAPTER 26

Let's burn this damn thing," Sarah said, her arms raised and ready to toss the Ouija board into the furnace.

"No, wait," Laine said, holding her back. "It won't work unless we do both together. You wait here while I..." She took a deep breath. "While I go and get the body."

She shone her flashlight down the passageway beside the furnace. It seemed longer today. Laine looked away to give Sarah a brave smile and looked back. There she was, DZ, blocking the passageway and grinning. Laine jumped, but when she looked back, the passageway was clear.

Suddenly the Ouija board blew out of Sarah's hands, flying upward into the air before sending her up with it. At the same moment, an unseen force knocked Laine across the room. Without thinking, she began to crawl toward the altar. DZ knew what they were doing, and she was fighting back. Sarah hit the ground hard, peeling her head upward to watch her sister disappear into the secret room.

"Laine," she muttered as the planchette flew through the air, landing inches away from her head, hitting the board. Sarah's arm jerked unnaturally and landed on the planchette.

"Sarah!" Laine screamed out, looking back as her sister's hand was dragged around the Ouija board, cycling through the same letters over and over and over.

D-I-E-F-R-E-N-D

"Sarah, let go!" Laine cried. "Let go of the planchette!"

"I can't!" Sarah cried out, her arm wrenching around in the socket, her wrist twisting and cracking into impossible angles. "Laine, help!"

Laine turned back toward the altar. There was only one thing she could do. She bolted across the room and grabbed DZ's mummified corpse. Her newly unstitched mouth lolled open in a grotesque smile. Grimacing, Laine carried the body carefully back to the passage.

Back by the board, Sarah was fighting against the pain in her arm. DZ's twisted ghost continued to push it farther and farther, inch by inch, waiting for the break. Sarah's eyes were closed and she bit down on her lip so hard she could taste blood.

"Hey!" Laine called out. DZ looked over but she did not let go of Sarah's arm.

"Let my sister go," Laine threatened, holding the body aloft.

"Laine," Sarah screamed and the sisters locked eyes for the briefest of moments, before she fought through the searing agony and pushed the board across the floor.

Without hesitation Laine heaved DZ's body

into the furnace. The flames crackled and popped around the mummified corpse before the fire consumed it completely.

At first there was only one scream. Then more and more voices joined the howl, rising up in an earsplitting, soul-shattering sound. Both girls covered their ears and dropped to the ground, the sound utterly overwhelming. Laine looked over at her sister and saw her eyes roll back in her head, blood beginning to trickle from her ears. Fighting against the agony, Laine grabbed hold of the board, determined.

But Doris was just as determined. The ghost of the girl soared across the room, arms outstretched and toes dragging across the floor. With one final scream of her own, Laine thrust the board into the furnace and braced herself, trying to shut the furnace door even as the flames leaped out, licking at her hands and arms, the burning sensation not nearly as painful as DZ's screams. Finally she slammed the door shut, just as DZ pounced.

A blast of energy tossed Laine across the room

like a rag doll. Her head slammed against the wall and she blinked at the scene before her: Sarah opening her eyes across the room and bright yellow flames roaring against the door of the furnace, thousands of dark, angry voices screeching into nonexistence.

And then silence.

Laine slumped down to the floor, her eyelids fluttering, like her flashlight. There in the middle of the room was DZ. Not the grotesque, black-eyed demon but just a little girl. Just Doris Zander, no stitches, no horror, no screaming. She smiled at Laine, thankful and sweet, and looked up, beaming as her mother reached out for her hand. The mother's face, so frightening before, was transformed with love. She took hold of her daughter and sighed. Love and relief. The pair smiled at each other, restored and reunited, and then they disappeared.

"Hi, friend."

Laine looked up. It was Debbie.

"It's you." Her voice was so weak, she could barely hear herself. "Am I..."

"Shh," Debbie said, smoothing her hair. "It's all okay."

Laine smiled weakly.

"Thank you," Debbie whispered, pressing her lips against her best friend's ear. "Good-bye."

"Good-bye," Laine replied. Her head hit the floor and Debbie was gone.

EPILOGUE

A photograph of Debbie, Laine, Trevor, Pete, and Isabelle sat on Laine's desk. The five of them looked happy, sitting around in the sunshine, arms draped around each other, and everyone was smiling.

Laine touched it carefully, just her fingertips making contact with the glass.

"Hey." Sarah knocked gently on her door. She was wearing her pajamas, face freshly scrubbed, all ready for bed.

"Hey, you," Laine replied, sitting on her bed.

"You okay?" Sarah asked.

Laine couldn't help but think her sister looked older. "Yeah," she said. "Yeah, I think so. I just... I miss them. All of them."

"Me too," Sarah said, entering her sister's room and sitting beside her, resting her head on Laine's shoulder.

"I guess you never really feel like you get to say good-bye," Laine said. "And maybe that's okay."

"Maybe there are no good-byes," Sarah suggested. "Not really. When I woke up on the floor, I saw, or at least I thought I saw..."

Laine looked at her sister, her eyes shining with hopeful tears.

"I saw all of them," Sarah said in a thick, quiet voice. "Trevor and Isabelle. Pete was holding Debbie's hand, like he always did. And they were smiling at us, Laine."

Laine smiled for the first time in a long time. She liked that thought, whether Sarah had really seen it or not. Sarah gave her sister a good-night hug and headed back toward her bedroom.

"Is it really over, Laine?" she asked, pausing in the doorway.

"Yeah." Laine nodded. "I think it is."

Sarah's face was still creased with sadness. "That poor girl," she said. "Where do you think they went, the spirits? When we broke the connection?"

Laine's smile faltered a little.

She didn't know.

Laine wiped the steam away from her bathroom mirror as she stepped out of the shower. Ever since Sarah had asked her what had happened to the spirits, she hadn't felt quite right. Grabbing the floss from the medicine cabinet, she watched herself in the mirror. *They are gone*, she told herself. The screams, the smoke, everything was gone. She pulled the floss away from her lips, quickly, tossing it in the trash and opening her mouth wide in the mirror to check her teeth.

Shaking her head and smiling to herself, Laine stepped back into her bedroom, fresh pajamas, fresh sheets, and in the morning, a fresh start.

Turning toward her bed, Laine froze, a scream stuck in her throat. She scanned the room but there was nothing, no one. Everything was exactly where she'd left it, apart from one thing.

Slowly, Laine reached out and picked up the planchette from the middle of her bed, turning it over in her hands. The weight of it, the smoothness of the wood. It really was there. It had found her.

Reluctantly Laine held the lens up to her eye and scanned her room...

YES

OU

ABCDEF

NOPQRS'

12345

GOOI

JA

NO

HIJKLM
UVWXYZ

67890

YE

YES   NO

GOOD BYE